"When did I tell

He hesitated jus~ ... ~nstant. iviust ve been the night after the guy was shot in your house."

I tried to remember that conversation and came up blank. In fact, I tried to remember when I had first recalled the smell.

It was the night of the marathon in Nevada. But then I had fallen asleep and forgotten it again until I got to Everly's house. I was certain I hadn't told Dad about it the night of the shooting in my house.

Ten minutes after I disconnected the call with Dad, I called Dave Jensen, chair of the school board.

We exchanged pleasantries for a few minutes, covered recent events in sports and politics, talked about his daughter's placing in a recent piano competition, and then I dropped the bombshell on him.

"I'm turning in my resignation."

He sounded like someone had just informed him of a death in the family. "Mike! You're kidding! Oh, my god! I can't believe it." Regaining his composure and wit, he asked, "Was it something I said? Something I did? Something I wore? I'll change it; I promise!"

"It's the color you dyed your hair. I just can't stand to look at it at the board meetings." I laughed and explained about the training. "I know it's a long shot, man. But if I don't try, I'll always regret it. I know I will."

In the end, he told me to go chase my dreams. And to bring a medal back to the old alma mater. Then he told me that the school attorneys were trying to reach me regarding an upcoming brief due in the Stoltz case.

After the call, Everly, who had come in a minute earlier, asked, "So you're taking Dad up on his offer? I thought you weren't deciding until tomorrow morning."

"I had to call my friend on the school board tonight. If I called him when I get up in the morning, he'd be really ticked off. Pacific Time Zone, you know."

Tapping the phone against my thigh, I said suddenly, "I need to find a place to live. I mean, a week is a favor. A week is a vacation. But permanent lodging is rent. Permanent lodging is overstaying one's welcome."

She made her little humming sound. Then she proposed, "Tell you what. If you will help me on the ranch for a couple hours a day when you aren't training, I would consider it rent."

I laughed. "Right. And just what can I do to help you on the ranch without causing you more work and getting myself maimed?"

"For one thing, you can carry fifty-pound bags, right?"

"Carry, yes. Trip and fall, yes. Where would I be carrying said bags, and how many of them are there?"

She explained that she had just bought a pallet (whatever that meant) of salt and a pallet of mineral. Apparently these things needed to be re-stacked in the machine shed.

"Shouldn't it be called a salt shed?" I asked.

She snorted. Then she said, "It's still light. Let's go."

After a few fits and starts, she decided I wasn't too handy at carrying bags. But I could stack them reasonably well (only two bags slid off the pile and landed on my foot). So she moved the awkward sacks from the back of the truck (pickup) to the salt room in the barn. After she handed them (tossed them) to me, I stacked them on a wood pallet that was designed to trip the able-bodied as well as the visually impaired.

It was past sunset when we finished stacking the bags. A coolness settled over the land as we climbed into her pickup. Driving down the dusty lane with the windows open was a delightful experience.

When we walked into the house, I realized I had left my phone there. It was buzzing, indicating a voice mail. I picked it up and played a message from Charles.

"Mike, alas, my heart is broken at the loss of my precious daughter. I'm sure you will understand why—and I pray will forgive me—for completely forgetting our scheduled runs last week. Please let me have another week before we resume our thrice-weekly runs. Blessings, my friend."

I responded, but was sent immediately to his voice mail. "Charles, please accept my heartfelt condolences. You and your family have been very much in my thoughts. I have, however, moved away from California recently, so I will no longer need a guide. Thank you for your help and friendship. Best wishes."

Minutes after I drifted into slumber that night, my phone rang. Mentally slapping myself for forgetting to shut it off, I reached for it and checked the Caller ID.

It was Dolores Stoltz.

I blocked the call and any further calls from the number.

The following day as Derek and I approached Everly's house on our return run, he told me Everly wasn't there.

"How can you tell?" I asked.

"Her truck isn't in the driveway."

I wagged a finger at him. "It's a pickup. Not a truck. Trucks have more than four wheels. Pickups have only four."

He laughed. His voice bobbing with his footfalls, he said, "You already got that lecture, huh? How about the cow lecture. Have you heard that one?"

"There's a cow lecture?" I pealed.

He replied, "Yeah. Did you know that not every animal that says moo is a cow?"

I considered the concept. "Well, you just said moo. And you aren't a cow."

"It has something to do with genders. As in, females are cows and males are bulls. Or steers. Something like that."

I winced at the term *steer*. "Why do they do that to them?"

"I don't know. But I'm sure Pacino can explain it to you."

"Pacino?" I inquired.

"Everly's nickname." He grinned. "She can explain that one to you, too."

"Hmm. Should make for plenty of conversation around the dinner table this evening," I observed.

"Supper table. You're in farm country, man. They eat dinner at noon. Supper at night. Took me a year to get that straight. Out of self-defense, I now say lunch and supper. That way everybody knows what I mean."

I gave him Everly's little, "Hm." Then I asked, "What does she look like?"

"Who? Everly?"

"Yeah," I returned. "I mean, she's my roomie, so I should have an idea. I know she's five and a half feet tall and slender. But I don't know if she's freckled and red-haired or green with yellow polka dots."

"She looks about like you," he responded.

I laughed. "No, really."

"Seriously. Her muscles are bigger than yours, and your chest is bigger than hers. Short brown hair. Blue eyes. I'm telling you, you two could pass for siblings."

"She doesn't look my sister," I said.

"How do you know?" he quipped.

"Because my sister is green with yellow polka dots. When we have family photos taken, we always have to be careful what we wear so we don't clash with her."

"Pacino's wiry," he elaborated. "Bony. Skinny. Look, I don't know if she owns a bra. And you can't tell from looking if she's wearing one. Absolutely no curves, if you know what I mean. Let's just say that if she did wear a bra, it might fit better backward than forward."

I was gasping for air. "You're horrible!"

"Not kidding," he returned dryly. "She looks as cold and unfriendly as she sounds, man."

"How old is she?" I inquired.

He thought about it a moment. "I really don't know. About our age, I guess. Late twenties. Early thirties."

"You don't like her," I pointed out. "Why?"

"Because she doesn't like me," he reasoned. "I didn't grow up on a ranch. Didn't grow up on a farm. Don't know how to drive a tractor or build a pig sty. I don't know a turnip from a radish, and I can't identify two breeds of cows. She's a country snob. No time of day for anyone who grew up in the city."

Bidding him adieu, I greeted the canine corps and made my way inside. In the kitchen, I downed a quart of chocolate milk.

Then I called Mom. We chatted for a bit, then I said, "Mom, if I show you Everly's pantry, will you tell me what's what?"

"Sure," she replied.

With the video app on my phone and Mom's interpretation thereof, I secured the necessary ingredients for a batch of burritos.

When dinner (supper) was cozily tucked into a warm oven to await its demise, I started my workout on the living room floor.

Between planks and crunches, I thought of something. Picking up my phone, I called Service Dogs of Central California.

Just checking, I said, to see if there is a dog for me yet.

The receptionist hitched. She said, "Um, just a minute, Mike. I'm gonna put you on hold. Okay? Just for a minute."

"Sure, no problem," I answered.

It was longer than a minute. I did a hundred sit-ups before she came back on the line.

"Mike, I'm going to have you talk to Tiffany, okay?"

"Thanks." I would have addressed the receptionist by name, but I'd forgotten it somewhere between fifty and sixty sit-ups.

Tiffany's familiar voice came on the line. "Hi, Mike. How are you today?"

"Great," I said. "I was just checking to see when you'll have a new dog for me."

"Well, I may have a little problem here. See, I got a call from someone claiming to be your dad. He said you had decided not to get a new dog just yet."

"Oh? When was that?" I asked deliberately.

"According to my file, he called us about three weeks ago. Which I thought was good timing because I actually did have a dog I thought would work for you. But we assigned him to another client. Is this a problem? I mean, was that really your dad? Because you sound as though you didn't know you had asked to wait."

I took a deep breath and let it out slowly. "No problem. Not on your end. Thanks, Tiffany. I'll let you know when I change my mind."

I disconnected and sat there staring blindly into space. Which I'm pretty good at.

Why would Dad have called off my replacement dog? Because he thought someone had murdered Harley?

It didn't make sense to me.

I left a message on Dad's phone and resumed sweating on Everly's living room floor.

When my host walked into her house, she said, "Hi. Didn't you learn that crunches are bad for you? Shouldn't you be wearing a face shield? And what is that heavenly smell? Did you order out?"

"I made burritos. I had to use a few substitutions. Couldn't find your cilantro. Is ordering out even possible here?" I panted.

"Not really. Maybe it is if you can drive." She passed through to the kitchen and opened the oven door. "Wow. Will these save for a little later? I need to check cows. I was hoping you might help me again."

Finished with the set, I hopped to my feet. "Sure. Love to. What do I need to do?"

She came back into the room and must have given me an appraising glance. "Put on some jeans if you have any."

I disappeared to my room and returned properly clad. Or so I thought.

"Those your only jeans?"

Hesitantly, I replied, "Yes."

"Hm."

"What's wrong with them?" I asked.

"Nothing if you don't plan to do any actual work. Why did you guys quit so early today?"

"Because we started so early. And because it was over a hundred degrees. Your dad very thoughtfully didn't want to kill us."

"Very thoughtful, indeed. It's not five yet. Let's take you to town and get you some real clothes."

Fifteen minutes later, we walked into a store that sold everything from horse feed (which smelled pretty good) to fence posts (which smelled pretty awful) to work clothes. Which smelled about like one might expect.

"Hey, Ev! What did you bring me?" came a sweet and very feminine voice.

Having left my cane in her truck (pickup), I walked in a step behind Everly, my left hand resting lightly on her right shoulder.

"Hi, Jeannie. This is Mike. He's from California, and he needs some real clothes." I noted a distinct difference in

Everly's voice. It sounded kind. Nice. Friendly. Not like it sounded when she addressed me. "Mike, this is Jeannie."

I stuck out my hand. "Hi, Jeannie."

Jeannie returned the handshake and said, "I think we can fix you up. What size do you wear, Mike? You look like about a thirty, thirty-six."

My brows shot up. "More like a thirty-thirty."

Everly said, "Not in work jeans. These will come down over your boots. Oh, and you need boots, too. But let's start with jeans."

Jeannie bounced around for a couple minutes selecting an array of things for me to try on, and then said, "Here you go."

I reached out and took two pairs of jeans, stiff as boards, folded into thirds. "Where do I go?" I asked.

"Right over there," Jeannie replied.

Everly started to say something, but Jeannie exclaimed, "Oh, my god! Are you blind?"

"Yep," I answered easily. "All my life."

"Oh, my goodness! Oh, my gosh. I didn't know! I'm so sorry," she squealed.

I smiled. "No problem. But I might need slightly more elaborate directions to the changing room."

She took my elbow and hastily led me ten feet before she ran me into a rack of shirts. Then she apologized again.

I regretted not being able to see how red her face was becoming.

When I emerged from the fitting room in the first pair of unbelievably rigid jeans, I could only move like a stick figure. Wearing what I hoped was a look of utter disbelief, I said, "I don't think this is the right size."

"Oooh!" Jeannie crooned. "Those look really good on you. Are those the twenty-nines or the thirties?"

"That's the right size," Everly evaluated. "Those are working jeans."

Wrinkling my face, I retorted, "I can't work if my circulation is cut off. And they're way too long."

"Not if you're wearing boots," Everly repeated.

Jeannie shrugged. Yes, I could hear her shrug. She was wearing a lot of jewelry and it clanked and tinkled. "He could maybe go up a waist size, but I think those are perfect. Of course, if he won't be on a horse, you could put him in bib overalls."

Not certain how I felt about them discussing me as though I were standing in another state, I said, "I don't think I could get on a horse in these. They don't bend."

"They'll soften up after a couple trips through the laundry. But he can't ride in overalls," Everly stated authoritatively. "He would chafe."

That didn't sound promising. After a moment, I hesitantly inquired, "What exactly would I chafe?"

Everly probably thought I didn't hear her attempt to suppress a snicker. "The insides of your knees. It would make running very uncomfortable for a few days."

I suspect my countenance expressed distaste.

Eventually they led me to the boot section.

I had never worn a cowboy boot in my life.

They were heavy, clunky, stiff, and with every step, my heel slid up and down inside them. "I couldn't outrun a one-legged cat in these things," I complained.

"You don't have to," Everly stated plainly. "They protect you from hooves and dropped tools and thorns and nails."

I shrugged. "Okay. I guess I'll get used to them. In about fifty years. Do they have to be so tall? They come almost up to my knees. And does the heel have to be so high? I feel like I'm sliding downhill with every step."

"The tops are high because rattlesnakes rarely strike above the knee, and the heel is high so your foot doesn't slide through a stirrup and get you hung up."

My face crinkled in horror. "Maybe instead of helping you on the farm, I'll just pay you rent. I'm not fond of rattlesnakes, and I don't like the sound of hanging up in a stirrup."

"You'll be fine," Everly assured me.

I didn't feel assured.

I handed over my credit card at the end of the outing and learned that the jeans were cheap. The boots, however, were startlingly expensive.

But having two women fuss over me in a clothing store was admittedly a lot of fun, whether I was on the East Coast or in the middle of the continent.

Back on the ranch, Everly stopped the pickup and stepped out. "Am I supposed to get out, too?" I asked.

She leaned into the open window. "No. I'm opening the gate. Sit tight."

I sat tight.

She got back inside, drove a few feet, and stopped again. Stepped outside. Got back in again.

"Did you have to shut the gate?" I asked when we were moving again.

"Yes."

"Is that something I could do to help out?" I inquired.

"It would take longer to show you how to open each gate than to do it myself." Half a minute later, she said, "But you could drive the pickup through."

Dryly, I said, "Darn, and I just recently let my driver's license expire."

"I'm not asking you to drive to town," she replied with equal dryness. "You just have to pull straight ahead about thirty feet. Have you ever driven at all?"

"I sat on the driver's seat when Dad replaced the brakes in Mom's minivan. When he said press on the brake, I pressed. He said let up, and I let up. That's the closest I've been." I managed a straight face for almost ten seconds.

Then, with a chortle, I admitted, "Okay, I did drive in a big parking lot once. But there was a lot of alcohol involved. No fatalities. No arrests. Just a lot of college-aged males having a really good time."

She turned toward me. "Did you make the tires squeal?"

I laughed harder.

As we approached the next gate, she began thinking aloud. "You can slide over here and. . . well, actually, you don't have to slide over here. It's not like you're already used to driving from behind the wheel. You could drive from there like the mailman does, right? Yeah. Let's do that."

"I'm not comfortable driving your car," I stated firmly.

"It's not a car. It's a pickup. And what harm could you possibly do? You will push on the brake and put it in gear. Then ease off the brake and gently apply pressure to the accelerator. Then when I say, 'Whoa,' you press on the brake again and put it back in Park."

"Hm."

She snorted at my use of her mantra.

I asked, "What exactly does your little hum mean?"

"Yes, no, and maybe so. We're at the next gate. So this first time, you slide over here behind the wheel."

"I don't think so."

"Come on," she said impatiently. "But don't let off the brake yet. I have to open the gate first."

A moment later, she was standing outside the driver's window. I was behind the wheel. She instructed me to hold the wheel steady. Press on the brake. I used my left foot. She told me to use my right foot.

I recalled Dad telling my siblings that. Always use your right foot.

Okay, well, if I were becoming a driver, I supposed I better do it correctly. So that later when I was good enough to start driving on the freeway. . . .

Brake on, I pulled down on the gear lever. Three clicks. Ease off the brake. Ease on the accelerator.

Wow! Too much gas. Or diesel. Whatever.

Focus on the *ease* part. Okay. Through the gate. We were moving. Everly was outside my window walking. I hoped I wouldn't run over her foot.

Okay, far enough. Gently press on the brake. Wow! Too much brake. Then three clicks up with the gear lever.

Pshew. Survived my first sober driving experience.

I slid back over to the more familiar passenger seat. The rest of the cow-checking was uneventful. I drove through three more gate openings. Amazing.

I also learned that mature cows are cows. Male cows are oxymorons. Intact males are bulls. Castrated (ouch) males are steers. Young females are heifers. Very young cattle of either gender are calves.

"What about the ones who aren't sure of their gender?" I asked with a straight face. "The ones who haven't decided yet with which gender they identify?"

She rewarded me with another snort. "This ain't California, buddy. In Nebraska, if there's a penis, it's a male. If there's a vagina, it's a female."

"Well, thank you. That should clear things up."

She turned toward me. "Do you have a question about your gender?"

I grinned. "I assure you I am absolutely certain which of those aforementioned parts I possess. No questions here."

"That's good," she mumbled. "After seeing what you called jeans, I wasn't sure."

Ignoring that, I observed, "You drive very smoothly. It's harder than it seems."

"The week I got my driver's license, Grandpa had hemorrhoid surgery. My job was to drive him around until he could drive himself. For a week, I got yelled at for ramming on the gas and slamming on the brakes. Which I didn't think I was doing. But in his condition, Grandpa sure thought so. So by trial and error and a lot of yelling, I learned to drive very smoothly. And thank you for noticing."

I returned to the prior topic. "So why do you make steers? Isn't that pretty cruel?"

"It's crueler when you go out in a pasture and find one of the bulls beat to hell because the other bulls tried to kill him." As she warmed to the topic, her voice rose in volume and intensity. "It's crueler to find a bull that's been gang-raped by a band of other bulls leaving him barely able to stand. It's crueler to find a bull dehydrated because he's afraid to go to the water tank because he's trying to avoid the other bulls. It's crueler to see a—"

Holding up a hand, I said, "I get the picture."

"Excessive testosterone causes a lot of problems," she added.

My face crinkled. "Let's talk about something more pleasant. Like global warming. Or terrorism. Or politics."

She replied, "Suit yourself."

"So have you lived here all your life?" I inquired. "I know you didn't live in Africa when Gunnar was coaching there."

"No. He came home for a month every year, and that's when we traveled. Looking back, I think he didn't really want to spend a month with his in-laws. Or with cattle. So we toured the world. By the time I graduated high school, I had been in forty-seven states, four provinces, and seventeen countries."

"Nice," I answered. "But otherwise, you've been here all the time?"

"I went to college in Indiana."

"Purdue?"

She didn't answer.

I tried again. "Purdue?"

175

"Oh, god. I'm sorry, Mike. Nodding to you doesn't cut it. Yes. I went to Purdue."

I smiled. "I consider it a compliment that you forgot just for a moment that I'm blind."

She seemed distracted.

I said, "It's rude to text and talk at the same time. Not to mention texting and driving."

"I'm not texting." With her head hanging out the window, she murmured, "Right now I wish you weren't blind. It'd be nice to have a second set of eyes to help count cows."

"Are you counting now?"

Again, she was slow to answer. "Yeah."

I waited.

"Okay. Sixty-three head. Perfect. We'll check the salt next."

I grimaced. "Does that require stacking bags?"

She turned toward me. "No. We'll just drive by the salt tub and see how full it is. Or isn't. Then we'll go eat your burritos."

"So after college, you came back here?" I asked.

"No. I worked for a year in Newark, New Jersey. Then Solomon, California."

"Solomon?" I enthused. "Solomon is my town! I grew up in Solomon. And that's where my school district is. Was."

"I know."

Grinning widely, I said, "That's cool. So what did you do there?"

"I worked for the government."

"That doesn't narrow it down much," I said dryly. "One in five people in this country works for the government. Technically, I worked for the government."

She did her "Hm" and added, "I'm no longer one in five."

176

I pondered that for a while. Then I offered, "You seem to have some degree of heartburn over people who didn't grow up in an agricultural community."

"Of course I do," she said, as though it were obvious.

"Why?" I pressed.

With a sigh which belied exasperation, she said, "All my cousins grew up in big cities. When I was a kid, I knew they were superior to me. I didn't know why. But there was always this little undercurrent to that effect even though no one ever said it aloud. And I never understood it, but I felt it, too. It just seemed like I was never quite as good, quite as civilized, quite as well-rounded as they were. And when I got older, I asked myself just what it was that they had that I didn't. My ACT scores were higher. My GPA was higher. Certainly my morals were higher. I never smoked pot. I was never drunk. Not one of them could saddle a horse or drive a tractor. All I could figure they had that I didn't have was a mall. So what the hell is up with that?"

I had no answer.

Back at the house, I listened to a string of emails from the school attorneys while Everly went to take a shower. If I'd had my way, I would have joined her.

But I didn't.

When I finished, I went to the refrigerator and drained the chocolate milk. A second after I tossed the empty jug in the trash can, Everly yelled, "Stop!"

I froze.

She blew out a deep breath. "I thought you were going to fall down the stairs."

My eyes popped open. "Stairs? You have a basement?"

She sighed again. "I'm sorry. I should've told you. You weren't about to fall, I guess. But I just came around the corner and you were there at the top of the landing. I suppose I should show you around down there. If you were home alone with a storm on the way, you'd need to go down to the cellar."

With my hand on her shoulder, I followed her down the stairs. The spacious and tidy first room contained a ping pong table. Around the corner was a storeroom.

It could have also been accurately called a labyrinth.

"Hang on," she grunted as she leaned down to slide some things out of the way. "Just a second. Stay right there."

"What are you moving around down there?" I asked.

"Boxes. Canned pinto beans were on sale, so I got a couple cases. And peaches. And pears. And creamed corn. I haven't put the cans on the shelf yet. If you ever need any frozen beef, the freezer is over here."

Standing erect once more, she led me through a narrow path toward the corner. Taking my hand, she put it on the handle of an upright freezer. She tugged open the door and indicated that the top two shelves were occupied by two-pound tubes of hamburger. Frozen corn and beans from the garden were on the next shelf. Below that was frozen pies.

"Pies?" I asked. They weren't in boxes like I would have expected from the market. These were in big plastic bags.

"Yeah. We make a bunch when the apples are ripe. Then when you want an apple pie later in the year, you just pull it out of the freezer and pop it in the oven. An hour later, voila. Fresh, hot apple pie."

"Sounds good. How about we bake one up right now?"

"It's too hot outside to run the oven," she said. "But I might set the timer to bake one early in the morning."

"What's this?" I asked when I felt the next shelf down.

"Steaks, mostly. T-bones. Porterhouses. Sirloin. Round steak. Flank steak. Flat irons."

"No kidding?" I emitted reverently.

"When I was a kid, I hated steak. Hamburger was easier to eat. But we had steak all the time. It wasn't until I was in high school that I found out some people go ape over steak." She pulled out two packages. "Here you go."

"Really?" I replied breathlessly as she placed two freezing, cling-wrapped parcels in my hands. There was nothing identifiable in their slightly cubical shape. They were merely frozen blocks.

"We better go upstairs before you get frostbite. Oh, there are some packages of nuts here, too. You want to have a bull fry?"

Wrinkling my lip, I hugged the precious beef morsels to my chest. "I'll stick with these. What kind are they anyway?"

"T-bones and filets."

"Filet?" I smiled. "I love filet! But these will be frozen for a while."

"We'll grill filets tomorrow and save the T-bones for the next day."

"Awesome," I emoted. As I was now closest to the exit, I led the way carefully back to the bottom of the stairs.

"It takes longer to get there when you're in front," she lamented.

"I could hurry, but you'd have to pick me up," I said as I slid each foot forward before shifting my weight to it.

Just as I set the steaks on the counter, my phone rang. According to the Caller ID, it was a California number. I didn't recognize it.

I shouldn't have answered it.

"Mike, you bastard! What the hell is wrong with you? Why can't you just stop screwing up my case? I know you're writing those damned briefs. They have your smell all over them!"

Letting out a deep breath, I sounded calm when I replied. "Dolores, you must not contact me directly. You need to go through your lawyer."

"Yeah? Well, screw him, too! He just keeps asking the same damned questions. Screw him, too! Whose side is he on, anyway?"

Without further ado, I disconnected the call and blocked the number.

"How many times has that happened?" Everly asked.

I jumped when she spoke. I had forgotten she was there, though she had likely heard every loudly slurred word. "I've lost count. Three or four. This one was from a new number."

"Are you going to notify her lawyer?"

"I'm going to notify my lawyer," I announced. "He can take it up with her lawyer."

At noon the next day, Shelley handed out dessert and then said, "Mike, there's something I've been meaning to give to you. I've been looking for them since you came, and I finally found them this morning. I'll be right back."

I was finishing the last bite of pie when she pulled out the chair beside me. Dropping a cardboard box on the floor, she sat on the chair and said, "Hold out your hands."

I complied. She handed me a book. A Braille book.

She said, "The front cover is torn off this one, so I have no idea what it is."

"Aha! A mystery. Let's see here." I found the title and held my left hand at the beginning of the line while my right fingertips slid quickly across the bumps. "Mystery solved. This is *Dark Canyon* by Louis L'Amour." I pronounced the author's first name *Lewis*.

Shelley immediately corrected me. Seems the name was pronounced *Louie*. "You haven't heard of him?" She sounded surprised.

I had not.

She explained, "My dad picked up these books at a farm sale years ago. I have no idea why. But they've been sitting around here forever, and I thought you might be able to put them to use. Louis L'Amour is the bestselling western author in history."

"I thought that was Zane Grey," I announced. "Or at least I've heard of Zane Grey."

"Both of them were good, though I have to say I find L'Amour's books to be more. . . I guess more reliable. Some of Zane Grey's books are to my liking. All of L'Amour's are. His books are still selling by the millions worldwide. So do you have any interest in reading these? Or should I just throw them out?"

"Hey, I live on a ranch now. I'll give it a try. I love to read. Anything with dots."

"Well, you don't have to read them if you don't want to. But I'll drop them off at your place. There are five or six of them here." I could hear her digging through her box.

"All novels?" I asked.

"I think so," she mused. "Yes. The others have the titles and authors written on the covers in pencil. Three Louis L'Amours and two Zane Greys. So you can compare the authors for yourself."

"Thanks," I repeated. "I'll start one tonight and let you know tomorrow."

Late that afternoon, I lay on the couch with the book propped on my lap. Everly walked through the room, stopped for a second near the doorway, and then chuckled.

"What's up?" I asked, my hands barely slowing.

"I was about to ask if you wanted the light on."

My hands stopped. I asked lightly, "But you didn't want to interrupt my reading?"

"Yeah. I guess it wouldn't bother you if it's on or off, would it?" She dropped onto the recliner. "I've never seen anyone read Braille before. Do you always use both hands?"

"I do when I'm speed-reading. If I'm just lolly-gagging or if the material is dry and tedious and requires more concentration, I use one—well, I still use my left to keep track of the line while my right reads. When I'm speed-reading, I read the first part of the line with my left, the rest with my right. Does that make sense?"

"More or less. How fast are you going? I mean, compared to a sighted reader. Because it looks like you're really flying."

"When I do the two-hand thing, I can read over three hundred words a minute. One-handed, I can only read about a hundred seventy. For comparison, most sighted readers read two hundred to two-fifty."

"What else can you do better than a sighted person?"

I shrugged. "There are a few advantages, I suppose. My ears are pretty keen. Not because I hear better, but because I pay more attention to what I hear. I have no trouble sleeping when the lights are on. It doesn't bother me when the windshield is dirty or wet or there's a glare. And you already know about the little tiny eyes in my fingertips. Some people who lose sight later in life are never able to learn Braille because their fingers have become calloused."

"I notice that your big round eyes don't have to point toward your little tiny ones," she prompted.

I was confused.

She elaborated. "When you are talking to me and doing something like washing your hands or folding laundry or tying your shoes, you turn your face toward me. When I do those things, I have to watch my hands. Well, I guess I don't have to. But I always do."

"How confining," I mused. A moment later, I observed, "Another advantage of being blind is that my eyes never play tricks on me."

"Ha," she responded with absolutely no humor whatsoever.

"Steep slopes don't scare me," I continued. "My sister is my favorite ski guide because she never forgets I'm blind. And she never gets sidetracked hot-dogging like Bryan does. But it always takes ten minutes to talk her into starting down the mountain for the first run of the day. She gets off the chair lift and looks down and gets scared.

"And I don't get seasick. Motion sickness is a mismatch between what one sees and what one feels in the inner ear. I can't compare the two, so I never get nauseous."

I noticed that night that she was right about me not watching my hands. As I sat at the piano playing around with a blues tune that had been floating through my head all day, I realized I was facing the piano with my right ear. Not with my face.

After an hour of piano, I buckled down and worked on the school board's brief in the Stoltz case.

When I woke in the morning, I slipped on my shoes and plugged in one earbud. On my way to the kitchen for coffee, I listened to the headlines. Nothing out of the ordinary in the international or national news.

But the headline on the front page of my hometown newspaper stopped me in my tracks.

"Former Superintendent of Schools Accused of Sexual Misconduct: Sandsebrotsky Resignation Admission of Guilt?"

I felt sick.

Accusations are often as good as conviction in public opinion.

The gist of the article was that Dolores Stoltz had expanded her accusations to include me. Her lawyer revealed in a press conference that I had not only tried to convince her not to press charges against Gregg Horst, but that I myself had molested her.

How had this ended up in the newspaper before I was notified? I sat down and sipped coffee and listened to the entire article. A search of the rest of the paper indicated there were no further related pieces.

For twenty minutes, I contemplated the wording of the email I would send to the school's attorneys. One of my questions to them was whether I should retain a personal lawyer. Another was whether they needed anything else from me in order to best represent the district.

Just before I drifted off that night, a text buzzed in. Ordinarily, I remembered to shut off my cell before bed, especially since most of my associates stayed up later than I and lived a time zone to the west. Suspecting that I would sleep better if I listened to the message before I doused the power, I tapped into it.

My dad's voice read, "From Charles. Rot in hell you f-ing pig."

With my heart pounding, I sat on the edge of the bed for several minutes. At some point, I was aware of Everly standing in the doorway.

"Did you hear that?" I asked.

"I think I did. But I thought I must not have heard it correctly. Mind if I look at it?"

I engaged the screen and handed her the device.

A moment later, I asked, "It did really say that, didn't it?"

With a sigh, she said, "In all caps. What do you know about this man?"

What *did* I know about him? I asked myself. I knew he was a follower of Islam. I knew he was an ophthalmologist. I knew he was married and had five children. I knew his oldest child had been murdered in my house, or at least her body had been placed in my house.

Before I answered, she said, "I hope you don't mind, but I'm scrolling up to look at your past messages from

Charles. He seems like a very kind and thoughtful man. This last message is out of character."

"Losing a child can do that to a person," I noted.

Pulling out her own phone, she asked, "What is his full name?"

I couldn't remember it. "It has a lot of z's and k's in it."

Dryly, she returned, "That's very helpful. Is he Middle Eastern?"

"Yes. From Iran. Zamo. . . no, Zana. Kamazi. Kazami. I can't remember. But you can find it, I'm sure. Just type my name in the search bar." I gave her the date of the shooting in my house.

"Wow. You're a famous guy. I got over twenty-seven hundred hits. Are these all you, or are there other Mike Sandsebrotskys in the world?"

"None that I know of. But every time I sign the minutes from a school board meeting, it's published. Every time I'm in a plane crash, it's published. Every time I win a race, it's published."

"Zana Kazemi. Sound right?"

"That's it," I returned.

She gave a low whistle.

"What?" I asked.

After a long sigh, she said, "This guy is a terrorist, Mike. Serious terrorist. As in, top ten wanted in the world."

Knowing that a top ten terrorist wanted me in hell was not a pleasant thought.

Checking my watch, I called Dad. No answer.

I forwarded him the text and asked him what he thought.

Chapter Seven
⠲⠄⠆ ⠐⠏⠶⠱ ⠠⠎⠈⠄⠈⠆⠆

On the way to Gunnar's house the following day—the day before the "training run" in Eastern Nebraska—I shoved thoughts of downed planes, terrorists, and rotting in hell to the back of my mind while Derek and I compared our pre-race and race rituals.

"The night before, it's spaghetti," I said. "With a little meat in the sauce, but not too much. Garlic bread. Tossed salad. Chocolate cake. Milk. How about you?"

"About the same. I like coleslaw instead of tossed salad. I don't know why. I think the acid helps my digestion or something. And instead of chocolate cake, I eat chocolate chip cookies. Oh, and gelatin. Fruity gelatin. And I'm careful about dairy before I run. Although it's probably okay the night before, I wouldn't touch it race morning."

We ran in silence for several strides.

"And a massage," Derek said. "I like a good massage the night before a race. Full body massage. That was Gunnar's suggestion."

"Who gives you the massage?" I inquired.

"My wife. But Shelley gave her some tips. And," he laughed, "Gunnar says he always raced better when he had sex with his wife the night before a race."

I scowled. "As opposed to sex with someone else's wife the night before the race?"

Derek laughed so hard he slowed for a couple paces.

When we were back on our stride, I said, "Dad hands me cool sweet coffee and marshmallows at six and twelve miles."

"I like a sports drink," Derek said. "And gelatin blocks, although that's nearly impossible when it's really hot like it will be in Sioux City."

We spent fifteen minutes discussing the race course. By then, we were at Gunnar's house.

Sitting at the breakfast table, we went over Gunnar's preferred "race eve" protocols. He mentioned everything Derek had said. Except the sex part.

"Mike," Gunnar said, "do you wear your glasses during a race?"

I explained, "I start with them. Sometimes I get so sweaty I can't keep them on. So I toss them right after I pass Dad. He picks them up."

"Run without them," Gunnar advised. "They'll just distract you. It's not like you need them. You aren't going to run into a sign post because you don't have them on, right?"

Gunnar was so serious that I tried to maintain a straight face. But I lost it. Derek cracked up, too.

"But never do anything different on race day," Gunnar stated.

"I haven't been wearing them lately when we're running," I said. "I carry them in my pocket and put them on when we get here."

"Well, they aren't necessary, right?" Gunnar pelted. "They don't protect you from sun damage or something, right?"

"No. I wear glasses to protect the rest of you. My eyes don't track together. I don't want to gross you out."

187

"Hell, I don't care," he snapped. "Your eyes could dangle down your cheeks by a thread for all I care. Ditch the glasses. They're too distracting."

"Okay," I snickered. Derek was giggling almost continuously now. "Shut up," I said to him.

He slapped my shoulder and let out a real guffaw.

"So, Gunnar," I began when I regained my composure, "because I'm staying with your daughter, I assume the race-eve ritual ends with the spaghetti supper."

"No," Gunnar said. "You should have a massage."

Derek started laughing again.

Perhaps because he decided we were a lost cause, Gunnar sent us home. We laughed most of the way.

As he climbed into his family minivan in Everly's driveway, Derek called, "Enjoy your spaghetti! Et al!"

"Et tu, Brute," I returned as I waved.

I tripped on the bottom step—thought it was at least six inches farther—and made my way inside. "Hi, Honey, I'm home," I called into what I thought was an empty house.

"You're early," Everly said, popping her head in from the kitchen.

"Oh, sorry! I didn't think you were here," I answered sheepishly. "Are we on cow patrol today?"

"It's race eve. Of course not. I'll cook the spaghetti when you start your shower. Which will be after your workout."

"Fabulous," I said. Crunches. Planks. Sit-ups. Push-ups. Stretches. Shower.

Spaghetti.

Halfway through the meal, I jerked up my head suddenly and said, "How are we getting to the race?"

"You're flying."

"Okay."

She continued. "In Derek's plane. It's a four-seater."

"What make and model?" I asked.

She snorted.

I pressed. "No, really. Why do you scoff? What make and model is it?"

"How would I know?"

I shrugged.

Instead of chocolate cake, she had made brownies for dessert. Even better.

After my third brownie, Everly stood and said, "Massage."

"Really?" I asked expectantly.

"Coach's orders."

She instructed me to lie on the living room floor. After I removed a small rock that had probably hitchhiked in on my shoe to end up under my shoulder, I relaxed and enjoyed the rubdown.

"So how's the ranching business these days?" I posed.

She let out a sigh. "Well, for one thing, Grandpa won't let go of the reins. He still wants to make all the decisions. On one hand, that's to be expected. He bought the place when he was twenty-two. Been working it ever since. But it's time he started allowing me to make some management decisions."

"Hard to let go," I garbled into the carpet.

"Yeah. I guess. He's eighty-eight years old. Today I told him that some people retire by that age. He said they were sissies."

"He's your mom's dad, right?"

"Right," she agreed.

"So you get hard-headed genetics from both sides of the family." I meant it to be light-hearted and hoped she would take it that way. She must have. At least she didn't take advantage of our relative positions and punch me.

After a full half hour of back, shoulders, and legs, she sat back and announced, "Done."

"Marvelous," I mumbled.

"Don't fall asleep there," she advised as she got to her feet. "You'll wake up sore."

I rolled onto my side and pushed myself to a sitting position. "Turn about is fair play," I said as I pointed to the floor. "Your turn."

She was silent.

I continued pointing. "Lie down. I'll give you a massage."

She was still silent.

I sighed.

Then she said, "Oh, I get it. You don't have any idea what I look like, do you?"

Grinning, I said, "You've checked me out since I got here. But I don't know anything about you." That was a lie, but she probably didn't know how much I could tell about her from the way she moved—not to mention from Derek's description. "Come on. Don't be so stodgy. Just lie down and enjoy a nice backrub. I'm told I'm quite good with my hands."

"That's what I'm afraid of." She swallowed. Let out a deep breath. After stalling for a full minute, she said, "Let me kick off my boots first."

I heard the boots. I also heard a belt buckle and wondered why she was removing it. But when I worked my way down her spine, I noticed she was still wearing a belt. She must have removed something that was normally attached to the belt. Phone case. Utility knife. Something that would have been uncomfortable to lie on.

I started along her spine. Worked her shoulders. She was lean and muscular, every rib pronounced. Derek hadn't been kidding when he'd said she was wiry.

"Wow!" I exclaimed when I got to her upper arms. "Flex." Circling her biceps with my fingers, I noted, "Twelve inches in circumference!"

190

Voice muffled by carpet and relaxation, she answered, "Twelve and a quarter on the right. Eleven and three-quarters on the left."

Resuming my work, I mused, "I don't know which is more disconcerting: the fact that your muscles are bigger than mine or that you know exactly how big they are."

"A couple years ago, I sewed myself a short-sleeved dress. The hem of the sleeves came to the middle of my biceps. But when I bent my elbow, the bottom of the sleeve rode up. So after that, I made sure to always measure the sleeve pattern before I cut it out."

"I don't know how you've managed to stay single around here if you can cook, sew, and shoe your own horse."

She made her little humming sound. Then she said, "I'll get married again when I find a man who's as smart as I am."

I snickered and said, "Roll over."

"What?" she snapped. I felt her tense.

"Facial massage. Very relaxing, I promise."

At least this hesitation wasn't as long as the original. When she was on her back and I was kneeling with one knee on either side of her head, I very gently began massaging her forehead, then her cheeks. My fingertips found a scar on her left cheek. I mused, "There must be a story with this."

"I got kicked by a cow when I was sixteen."

"Were you wearing glasses?" I asked.

"Yes," she replied. "The lower frame cut my face. It bled like crazy."

"Eight stitches?"

Disbelieving, she said, "Someone told you that."

"No," I parried. "I can feel the tiny dots where the stitches were."

191

"That's amazing," she murmured. After a while, she asked, "How do children learn to read Braille anyway?"

"My dad made a set of wood blocks similar to the ones other kids use. On each face, there was a regular letter carved in relief along with the Braille. Braille uses a matrix of six dots, two across, three up and down. Some of the dots stick up on the paper and some don't. But so that I would recognize that there were always six possible dots, he carved the blocks so the stick-up dots were in relief, and the non-dots were divots. My siblings also learned to recognize Braille, by the way."

"Do they read it with their finger or their eyes?" she asked.

"Eyes, apparently." My mind drifted momentarily back to childhood. "I remember very seriously telling Mom that something was wrong with Bryan because he couldn't read the letter on the back of the block. She explained to me that he was reading with his eyes. I didn't really get it at the time."

She gave her little hum. "You were reading the front letter with your thumb and the back one with your fingers."

"Exactly. And I hated to be the one to inform Mom that Bryan was retarded or something, but I knew she had to be told."

"So from blocks, you moved to books?"

"Right. The same kind of books other kids use except mine had a raised shape and enlarged Braille that said 'triangle' or 'square'. And I had a book with fuzzy animals and one with houses and fire trucks and one with airplanes. And Dad got me lots of models of all kinds of animals and vehicles and monuments. I have a six inch tall United States Capitol. Empire State Building. Jefferson Memorial. Eiffel Tower. It's much easier to learn their shapes when you can hold the whole thing in your hand. It would take me a lifetime to feel up the whole Eiffel Tower. All done."

Everly sat up and leaned her back against the couch. "Thanks for the backrub."

"You're welcome. Oh, wait! I just figured it out. Your nickname Pacino. Scarface. Is it that noticeable?

"Yes, unfortunately, it is."

"Doesn't bother me a bit. Dad says scars give people character. At least he told me that after the second time I got hit by a car."

"Good night," Everly said.

"Good night." I gathered my shoes and socks and padded toward my room. Apparently, any remaining race-eve ritual was up to me.

Just before I reached the door to my room, I stepped down on something squishy that squeaked. I let out a reflexive whoop.

Poking her head around the corner, Everly asked, "What the hell was that?"

"You tell me," I grumbled. "It felt like a mouse, but it was louder."

She flicked on a light switch and, trying to withhold a chuckle, said, "It's a cat squeaky toy. The cats drag them all over and leave them on the floor. Sorry."

From her tone, it was obvious that she wasn't really. Apparently, my impending heart attack was of no concern to her.

/

Chapter Eight

⠠⠹ ⠏⠌⠻ ⠠⠑⠊⠛⠭

Derek's plane was a Cessna 182. As I climbed into the back seat, I commented that it was just like one Bryan had taken me up in once.

"But he gets to fly bigger, faster stuff now," Derek lamented. "I've never gone past a single engine prop."

"That's because instead of a career in the Air Force, you chose to go run your guts out every day," I said flippantly as I ducked into the back seat.

"Running is better," Gunnar stated as he buckled his lap belt. "Don't crash."

Derek chuckled. "I'll do my best."

"Is it harder to fly when it's dark?" I asked.

"Nothing to it. The towns along the interstate look like little islands of light. Almost like a string of pearls," he said. Then he barked, "Clear!" to alert any passersby before he started the engine. Leaning over the back of his seat, he said, "Here are your Mickey Mouse ears. You're on Comm, so anything you say can and will be heard up here in the First Class Business Section of the aircraft."

I took the headset. "As long as the coach section lands at the same destination as the Business section, I'm satisfied."

"Next stop North Sioux City, America," he said as he urged the little craft down the taxiway toward the end of the runway.

"Is that in Nebraska or Iowa?" I asked.

"South Sioux City is in Nebraska. North Sioux City is in South Dakota. And Sioux City is in Iowa," Derek instructed. "There will be a quiz later."

"I'll study," I promised.

Not another word was spoken until Derek talked to the flight control tower on approach.

As we glided toward the runway, Derek asked, "Everybody still buckled?"

We both replied that we were.

Then the Tower came on and said, "Seven-Seven, keep your in-house checks in-house."

"Sorry, Tower," Derek said. I heard a click to indicate he had switched his mic to broadcast his voice only inside the plane and not to the rest of the world. Then he chuckled. "I guess the air traffic controllers don't need a reminder to get buckled to their chairs."

Gunnar said, "I hope you focus better on running your race than on running your radios."

"Yeah," I agreed. "And on landing the airplane."

"You know the definition of a good landing?" Derek pealed as he eased back the throttle and applied another notch of flaps.

"Any landing you walk away from," I responded.

Gunnar cleared his throat. It was a sound I had come to know. It meant he wanted us to focus.

But I wasn't sure if he wanted us focusing on the upcoming race or the upcoming landing.

We took a cab to a place a mile from the starting line, and then we lined up three abreast—with me in the middle—and jogged toward the place where the race would begin. Once there, Derek and I stripped off t-shirts and sweats and sat on the ground to switch from our running shoes to racing flats.

Gunnar looked down at me. "Mike, why are you wearing that vest again? It's gonna be too hot for that."

"I have to in a race," I stated. "I'm pretty sure it's in the rules. Are there other blind runners here?"

Impatiently, he snorted, "Hell if I know." Then he walked away.

When our flats were laced and double-knotted, Derek started fiddling with the tether. "Mike, what if we clipped these around our wrists or our elbows?"

He tied a thin strip of leather loosely around my wrist and clipped the tether to it. As he worked, he mumbled, "This was Pacino's idea."

Gunnar was back. "I don't like anything new on race day. You should do that kind of stuff at practice."

Derek, who had known his coach far longer than I, ignored him.

I asked innocently, "Isn't this just a training run?"

Gunnar chewed his fingernails.

A few minutes later, after we had run a block to see how the newly arranged tether worked, Derek pointed out, "Gunnar gets pretty hyped up."

"So do we," I reminded him.

"But we won't hear another word from him now. Once he walks away from the start, he's mum until the dissection at the end."

"Really?"

"Really. He'll hand me water, but he won't say a word. He might say something to you just so you'll know where to reach for your water. But he says coaching should be done at home. He only said something about the tether because he hates to try something new on race day."

"Even though it's only a training run," I grinned.

Derek chuckled. "Right. Hey, Paul Stuebbens is at two o'clock. I don't think he'll approach us before the race. Gunnar snapped his head off once for distracting me at the starting line. Paul's sure staring at you. Probably because you cleaned him in that last race."

"He ran well," I said.

Derek snorted. "You're too nice. Let's go."

Untethered, we found a set of Porta Potties. Then we made our way to the start and stood jumping up and down, bouncing on our toes, keeping our muscles warm.

Shortly before the starter began the pre-race instructions, Derek noted softly, "There are some other blind runners. And some in wheelchairs. I've never noticed those folks before. There must be about thirty of them. They all have on matching t-shirts. Achilles International."

"Over to the far side and behind everyone else?" I prompted.

He didn't respond. Then he said, "Oh, sorry. Yes."

Grinning, I asked, "Did you nod?"

He sniggered. "Yep"

Finally, the starter stepped into position and raised his gun.

Derek turned to me and whispered, "Let's go do some quality klurging."

The gun fired, and we were off.

Purposely, we stayed on the edge of the pack. Then we began passing the jackrabbit runners. Between miles two and six, we must have passed three hundred of them.

On most morning runs, Derek and I talked constantly. But not today. Today, there was radio silence.

Until Mile Thirteen.

"Mike," Derek panted easily, "does this seem downhill to you?"

"Definitely. One percent grade, I'd say. How's it look?"

"Downhill. Definitely downhill."

197

I could hear another runner near us. And I could feel the incline under my feet. We were climbing.

And we were playing mind games.

As we neared the footfalls of the other runner, Derek started whistling. I came in with a harmony.

"Good luck, guys," the other runner gasped as we passed him.

"Oh, hi," I said. "Hey, Derek, there's someone out here with us."

"Yeah. It's Doug Clark. Hi, Doug."

Soon, Derek could no longer hold back. He giggled for the next hundred meters.

As we neared the nineteenth mile, I suddenly heard a familiar voice ahead and to my right. To my left, Derek said, "Looks like the plane made it on time. There's your sweet coffee and marshmallows."

I broke into a wide grin and reached out to take the cup from my dad. "Thanks, Pop!"

"Go get 'em." He read off the elapsed time and gave an appreciative whistle. Behind me now, I heard him yell, "Hell of a run!"

Mind whirring with calculations, I emoted, "Derek! We're averaging four-fifty-nines!"

"Sure we are. What did you expect? This is great klurging, right?"

I laughed and broke my no-profanity rule. "What the hell is klurging, anyway?"

With a grin, he said, "We're using our sense of horkel. Blig, flang, and klurg. Don't you remember? It was your analogy, you know."

I chuckled. "Shut up and run."

Even at Mile Twenty-Two I felt great. Usually by now I felt dead. A good dead. But dead.

"Forty miles. . ." Derek mused. "This is only twenty-six point two. It's a cake walk."

198

Two miles later, Derek said, "Hey, Mike. Looky here."

My eyes had been closed. I opened them and said, "What am I looking at? Descriptive audio for the visually impaired, please."

"You're looking at the back of Paul Stuebbens. Nice race, Paul. You're looking good."

"Thanks," puffed the front runner.

"See you later, Paul," Derek said.

"Maybe not," Paul retorted as he kept pace with us.

"Man, I can't wait to get to the finish," Derek grinned. "My wife is four months pregnant. And you know what that means."

I thought about it for a while. "It means you're going to have another baby in five months."

"Yeah. But it also means she's in the second trimester. Ooh, la, la!" He looked over at me. Must have read the empty expression. "She's hot, man! She can't get enough! She's all over me all the time. She promised we could get it on as soon as we find a private place after the finish line."

"Oh," I answered knowingly. Really, what I mostly knew was that nobody was thinking about sex after running twenty-four miles.

More mind games.

"So when are you going to introduce me to her sister?" I begged. "So I can experience this second semester phenomenon, too."

"Trimester," Paul chimed. "You said semester. You meant to say trimester."

I laughed. "Occupational hazard. I've been counting down life by semesters since I was five years old."

The three of us ran together for a quarter of a mile. The only further words spoken came from Derek when he growled, "*Get over!*"

Later he told me that Paul was angling to trip me. But after Derek's admonition, he moved over a couple feet.

Then we left him and ended up finishing more than a minute ahead of him.

Instead of running an extended cool-down as I would have done in the past, I slowed with Derek. We walked big circles in the flat, open, empty block beyond the finish line. I gave Dad a hug.

Gunnar had met us at the finish and talked quietly until Paul Stuebbens stumbled across the line and staggered to his knees. A team of people apparently hired for the purpose trotted toward him and began to administer oxygen and otherwise fuss over him.

Previously, I had only heard about this part of Paul's routine because I was usually running a cool-down by the time he finished.

During Paul's drama, Gunnar amped his volume to be heard over the melee and clapped one hand on Derek's shoulder and one on mine. "Good job, boys. Good training run. We'll finish our workout later."

We didn't see Gunnar again for an hour—allegedly because he didn't care for Paul Stuebbens. Derek had told me during our run one day that Paul had practically begged Gunnar to train him. Gunnar had turned him down despite an offer to pay nearly four times the going training fees.

"Why?" I had asked.

"Because Paul has a lot of natural talent and a lot of money."

I had let it drop that day. Now, as we walked our cool down, I quietly asked for elaboration.

Derek looked around to make sure no one could overhear us before he explained, "Gunnar doesn't run or train runners for the money. You know how he says that ninety percent of running is between your ears and the other half is your legs and lungs? He says Paul relies too much on his talent. He's not willing to work. I asked Paul once about his average mileage. He says one day a month he runs twenty miles. His average weekly is seventy miles. You can imagine what Gunnar thinks of that."

Derek and I had averaged double that since I'd arrived in Nebraska.

As we walked, I suddenly felt as free as I had ever felt. No job. No paperwork. No squabbles between students, parents, teachers, staff, administrators.

Free!

Except for an upcoming case management conference regarding the Stoltz case and my upcoming testimony in another case.

Dad fell into stride with us and we chatted absently about family and hometown politics. He pressed a pair of sunglasses into my hand, and I slipped them on. "Thanks."

"I talked to Gunnar yesterday," Dad said. "He asked me to give these to you at the end of the race. And he okayed the coffee and marshmallows."

"Good. Thanks."

"Are your eyelids sunburned?" Dad asked.

"No. I've been running without glasses a lot. So I have a good tan now. Nothing like the burn I got in that last race."

"You ran almost six minutes faster today," Dad pointed out unnecessarily. Pride evident in his voice, he added, "I knew with a good coach you could improve. I didn't know it would be so soon, but I knew you had it in you."

Paul Stuebbens, apparently finished with his finish line histrionics, approached to turn our little trio into a quartet. But, having unclipped the tether long ago, Derek faded away from the conversation and returned us to trio status.

"I feel really honored to have had a chance to run with you four times now," Paul said.

"Handshake," Dad told me.

I stuck out my hand and, as I searched my brain to come up with four races in which I'd competed against Paul, said, "Thanks. Same here. You're a great runner."

"Thanks. So what kind of workout do you have later today?" he inquired, alluding to Gunnar's earlier flippant comment.

"I'm not sure," I said, playing it safe. "How about you?"

He laughed. "I'm going to sit next to the pool and drink a six-pack. And as soon as I can move, I'm gonna eat a couple steaks. Hey, do you ever get out to Colorado?"

"I think I changed planes in Denver once," I quipped. "That's about the extent of it."

"I have a cabin up in the mountains. You're welcome to use it anytime," Paul offered affably.

"Thanks," I replied. "That's very kind of you. How often do you make it up there?"

We chatted for a while about his vacation house. Most of the time, he said, it sat idle. But he said the next few weeks would provide the best whitewater rafting and hiking and reiterated that I was welcome anytime.

After another handshake, we parted with me promising that I would try to make it to the cabin sometime.

A minute of silence passed between Dad and me. Then he said softly, "He's an interesting sort."

That was vague. I asked, "In what way?"

"His eyes are cold."

"He sounds like a nice enough guy," I observed. "Gunnar doesn't care for him. Nor Derek, for that matter."

Dad looked over his shoulder at the departing runner and grunted noncommittally, "Yeah."

An hour later, to my immense surprise, I found myself sitting at a banquet table with Dad, Derek, Gunnar, and three representatives from Simpson Sports Syndicated. The table was covered with free samples and paperwork.

Simpson had started as, of all things, a chicken feed company and had moved into human supplements and nutrition drinks for the elderly and immune compromised. Now they also sold sports drinks and protein bars.

And they wanted to sponsor Derek and me!

We left with handshakes all around and promises that we would have a lawyer look over the contract and let them know within the week.

To my even greater surprise, we then had a similar meeting with representatives from Getcher Sports Gear Company. Both companies promised to not only use our images in advertising but to supply as much of their products as we needed in our training.

And money. There was money on the table, too. A pretty nice chunk of it.

Our cab dropped off Dad at the commercial terminal and then took us to the general aviation side of the airport. Gunnar jabbered nonstop, interspersed occasionally by a light-hearted quip from Derek or me. It wasn't until we were driving back to Gunnar's place after the flight that Derek and I broke into fits of post-race giggles.

The next morning, Derek was still exuberant over the race. He trotted up on the porch just as I was walking out the door, grabbed me in a bear hug, and then shook my hand.

"Man! That race was so great! I can't believe we both hit our PRs yesterday. And Gunnar called it a training race!" he bubbled. "A *training* race!"

As we stepped off the porch, I said, "It was definitely a best time for me— by a lot— but you ran faster in Barcelona last year."

"No, I didn't. I mean I did, but ten days after that race, they nullified all the records. Someone complained that the course was short, so the officials re-measured. Sure enough, it was two hundred eighty meters short."

"You're kidding," I spluttered. "I never heard about that."

"I think they were pretty shamefaced," Derek explained. "It was kept awfully hush-hush. There was a little tiny blurb about it in *Runner's World,* but that's all I ever saw. I gotta tell you, I was crushed. I thought I had really made a breakthrough."

"Well, we shattered it yesterday," I enthused. Just then I realized Napili was trotting alongside me. I slowed and said, "I'm not sure this pooch is supposed to be running with me today. His boss might need him at work."

We stopped, and I pulled out my cell phone. "I better give her a call."

"Hang on," Derek said as he peered back toward the house. "She says we can take him with us."

I stood rubbing the big dog's head. "What do you mean?"

"She's standing on the porch. I pointed at the pooch, and she waved us on."

Scowling, I asked, "Does she always stand around and watch us run?"

"Beats me," he shrugged.

As we picked up the pace again, I pondered aloud, "Ever noticed that Everly's animals all have Hawaiian names?"

"Probably because they lived in Hawaii when she was a kid," Derek stated. "Shelley once told me that Everly was practically fluent in Hawaiian when they moved back here."

I scowled. "Really?"

"Sure. Before Gunnar coached in Synghalia, he coached for some college in Hawaii for a few years. Maybe it was a high school, but I think it was a college. Pacino would've been about eight or ten."

We jogged in silence for almost a mile. Then Derek said suddenly, "Mike, I don't want to get all mushy and sentimental, but I gotta tell you, you've made me a better runner. Last year when Gunnar first started talking about recruiting you, I figured you would slow me down. I thought I'd be leading you around. But I've gotten better running with you. A lot better."

"Well," I reasoned, "it's always hard to run faster when you're in front. Better to have someone who can push you to train harder and get better."

"I never would have guessed that that someone would be a blind guy. But thanks, man."

"Thank you." I chuckled. "And right back at'cha. I never could have run that well before I met you and Gunnar."

Derek started to say something else as I asked, "Is it sunny or cloudy? I can't tell."

"High, thin overcast," Derek replied.

I thought about that for a while. "What does that mean? Is it cloudy or sunny?"

"Both."

"What?" I yipped. "Which is it?"

"It's both. There is a high, thin layer of clouds. I can see the sun through them, but it's not as bright as it would be if they sky was completely clear."

Flummoxed, I said "I don't understand. How can you see through a cloud? Clouds are opaque. They block the sun. So you can't see the sun through them."

He took a couple deep breaths before he answered. "Think of a screen on a window. It lets air pass through, right?"

"Sure."

"But not mosquitoes. Right?"

I made a growling noise in the back of my throat.

He laughed. "What is that? The sound of confusion?"

205

"You just altered my universe," I grumbled.

"That's amazing. Something that is common knowledge to a sighted child that blows your thirty-year-old mind. You didn't know clouds can be so thin?"

"Nobody ever told me," I said. "I know that cumulus are like cotton balls. Nimbus carry precipitation. Stratus are like a blanket. No one ever told me there are see-through clouds."

"How the hell did you teach science if you don't know about high, thin overcast?" He was silent for almost ten seconds before he cracked up laughing. "Actually, I didn't know the name for it until I took pilot training. I knew what it looked like, of course. But I wouldn't have known it was called high, thin overcast. Are you going to be okay, or do you need an ice cream cone to get over this revelation?"

I muttered, "I'd slap you if I didn't think you'd abandon me out here in the desert. Clouds you can see through. . . just boggles the mind, you know?"

There was another long stretch filled with only the sounds of nature and our feet hitting the ground, our lungs rhythmically filling and expelling. Recalling that I'd interrupted him, I asked, "What were you going to say?"

Dryly, he said, "I was going to tell you I've been training better because you're so upbeat. But that was before your daily lesson in meteorology."

I chuckled.

"Seriously, though. You're never down, man. You know Gunnar says ninety percent of running is done between the ears. Running is hard. It's hard work. And having someone to run with is a real blessing."

"You aren't going to kiss me, are you?" I posed.

He laughed.

A few minutes later, he asked, "What's your prediction for the new Speaker of the House?"

I didn't answer for a while. "I don't think we should talk politics."

"Why not?" he implored. "We talk about everything else."

"Because I feel vulnerable. You might run off and leave me out here in the middle of nowhere. Leave me to wander. To starve. To be ravaged by wild animals."

"Napili will protect you," he replied gravely. Then, lighter, he jabbed, "What kind of politics are you dishing out that are so objectionable?"

I stated, "My views are perfectly logical and orderly. But I'm here in the middle of the country where you people cling to your guns and religion. Heck, I'd never been to a church service until I came here."

"And you don't have a gun collection?" he asked innocently.

"I can disassemble and assemble a .357 faster than you can," I taunted.

"I'll take you on in a target match," he offered.

"Perfect. I'll meet you ten miles away from town at three o'clock in the morning during the next new moon."

He laughed. "Look, I know you're in the education system, which automatically dubs you a liberal. And I know you're from California, so you're doubly cursed. But are you one of those West Coast idiots who think that people can decide whether they want to be male or female? You think kids should be on their parents' insurance until they're fifty? You think we should give amnesty to all the illegal aliens?"

"Yes."

He howled with laughter. "No, really."

"Really," I said with a straight face. "And besides that, I think the government should provide free health care, marital counseling, transportation, cell phones, housing, hair care products, tickets to the opera, and blue jeans with those faded places on the thighs."

"Okay, but how do you think the race will come out for Speaker?"

"Sunny," I replied.

"Sunny? What does that mean? You think the lady from Florida will get the vote?"

"Look, a good friend of mine recently dubbed me a left-wing dingbat. And he's my friend. And," I added, "he's a school teacher in California. So if *he* thinks I'm a leftist, you would think I'm a communist."

"Communist or socialist?"

I sighed and shook my head. "How 'bout them Dodgers?"

He laughed. "I'll get you to debate politics. You'll see. And I'll make a convert out of you. Make a real man out of you instead of a girly-man."

To change the subject and convince him I wasn't girly, I asked, "Do you know Andrea Cabel?"

"Works at the bank," he supplied.

"I've talked to her after church a couple times. She seems nice. Is she married?"

"Whoa! Wow, Mike, this is where sightlessness can get you into trouble."

"Why? Is she ugly?"

"She's pushing sixty, dude. Her ovaries are shriveled like raisins. No future in that one."

It took me nine strides to formulate my reply. "Do you think that dating is purely an interview process to find a wife?"

"Don't you?"

I guffawed. "No way. First, it's an interview process for sex. If everything goes well, then maybe you move on to the next stage."

"You fruit loop," he admonished. "Do you want to take a guess as to when Tish and I had sex the first time? I'll tell you. It was eight hours after I slipped a ring on her finger and said, 'I do.' And it was in Room 226 at the motel on the west side of McCook, Nebraska, because I didn't want to wait all the way to the place I had booked in Denver."

"Please don't divulge any further details of the encounter," I pleaded.

After a minute of steady running and steady breathing, he said, "Really, Mike, if you want to interview someone, why don't you interview one of Andrea's two ex-husbands here in town and find out what nice guys they are. Man, there's some reason she drove them both to divorce court."

I made Everly's little humming sound. Then, just for kicks, I asked, "Do you think Everly's ever had sex?"

He chuckled. "Pacino? You've met her ex. Sperry. He's a pretty good-looking guy according to my wife. Arms like tree trunks. Perfect hair. Perfect skin. Stupid bastard."

My voice laced with innocence, I asked, "Do people really turn green when they're jealous?"

He slapped my arm. "You idiot! I'm not jealous of him. Just because he looks like a freakin' movie star. I can outrun him!"

For the next half hour, I bored Derek with the outline of the petition I was composing for my counter-suit against Dolores Stoltz. To my surprise and delight, his well thought out questions helped me clarify a few points.

The following morning at breakfast, I reminded Gunnar that I would need to spend a week in California to meet with people at the school to help transfer the helm to the new superintendent. I also had to testify in a court case and meet with the school attorneys regarding the upcoming case management conference in the Stoltz case. And my folks were celebrating their thirty-fifth anniversary. I was expected to help with the party.

"What is your role in party preparation?" Shelley asked as she dropped a pair of pancakes on my plate.

"Writing a check to my sister," I joked. "And I think she is expecting me to do something else. But I won't be volun-told about it until my arrival."

Derek chuckled. "Volun-told. I like that. Are you sure you've never been married?"

Gunnar stewed about my impending trip for most of the day. By the next morning, he had devised a training schedule for me to follow while I was away. He asked, "How are you traveling there? Not flying, I hope."

"Why not?" I asked. "I flew here."

"You don't have a good rapport with commercial aircraft," he stated with all seriousness.

I grinned. "I've been on a thousand flights. Only one of them crashed."

Gunnar asked, "Why don't you drive?"

I think my mouth actually physically dropped open.

Shelley made a save. "I think he means why not have Everly drive you."

To my surprise, Everly was fine with the idea of driving me to California. We made arrangements and talked about a few things we'd like to see on the trip out and back.

That night, I had a very non-platonic dream about Everly Galloway. Never one to put any stock in dreams, I nonetheless woke feeling quite certain that I would marry her someday. Odd, considering I'd never even kissed her. I had flirted a little. But she wasn't highly amenable to flirtation. She had inherited a deep streak of seriousness from her dad. Derek informed me that his father-in-law said Gunnar's late dad had been just as single-minded. Apparently it was an inherited trait.

The following afternoon was occupied by a photo shoot at Gunnar's place. The execs from Getcher and Simpson had pooled their resources and hired a single photography firm that took a million pictures of us in the weight room, on the track, in Shelley's backyard garden gazebo, and out on the lonely trail where we spent most of our days running.

In the second hour of shooting, one of the photographers quipped, "Derek, no offense. But I can tell you've done this before, Mike."

"Modeling?" I asked.

"Sure," she replied. "You know the lingo."

I nodded. "I did some modeling in college."

Derek stared at me. "Are you kidding? What did you model? Bikinis?"

Scowling, I begged, "With this puny runner's physique? I hawked suits, ties, and sport coats. I'm not built like Sperry, the ex. No big muscles. Nobody wants to see me in a swimsuit."

"How about sunglasses?" the photographer appealed.

I hesitated a second, wondering if that was a pure guess on her part or if she had done her homework.

Before I answered, she laughed. "I found your portfolio online. I've heard that company pays their models pretty well."

Recalling my experience with the sunglass company, I knew she had indeed done her homework. They had paid almost four times what I got for peddling suits and ties.

On the way back to Everly's place after Sunday dinner (lunch) at her folks, I asked, "What's on the cow schedule for the rest of the day?"

"It's the Sabbath," she said, as though that explained everything. "We rest."

"Oh," I responded. "So that means we sit around? I have to tell you, I'm not very good at sitting still."

"That's too bad. Because I was going to saddle a couple horses so we could sit together for an hour or two."

Dressed in my riding jeans and clunky boots and a smelly t-shirt that I had almost demoted from my running wardrobe to the rag collection, I climbed into the pickup. Napili hopped in and tried to sit on my lap. There wasn't quite enough room for both of us in the bucket seat.

My horse was introduced to me as Honu. Everly asked for my hand and placed it flat on the big animal's head.

Even if I had tried, I would not have been able to quash the smile that engulfed my face as I held my hands on the massive animal who stood patiently while I traced the short, fine hairs on his forehead. "He has a cowlick right in the middle of his face."

She wasn't completely successful in hiding her giggle. "That's called a whorl. He has one there between his eyes and one behind each ear. We'll get to ears in a minute."

She directed me down to his nostrils, chin, lips, and muzzle, and then back up to eyes and around to ears. I felt his jaw, his throatlatch—which is at the bottom of where his head and neck meet—the whorls behind his ears, his long, silky neck and coarse mane, withers, shoulder, barrel, croup, hip, stifle, and tail, the hairs of which were even longer and coarser than those of his mane.

Then she had me run my hands down the front leg. Forearm, knee, cannon, fetlock with its little tuft of hair on the back, pastern, coronet, and hoof. We did the hind leg also. Gaskin, hock, cannon, fetlock, pastern, coronet, and hoof.

"So below the knee or hock, everything is the same?" I asked. Then I interrupted my own question. "Except that the back cannon is longer than the front one."

"That's right. Most people don't notice that. I guess it's more obvious in Braille," she said. Then she picked up his front foot and demonstrated the sole, the frog, the sulci, and the bulbs.

"I'm sorry," she apologized as she set the foot back on the ground. "You probably didn't want a tour of the entire horse. It's just that I find these critters so fascinating."

I smiled. "Everly, please don't ever feel bashful about teaching me something. The minute I stop learning, I hope someone plants me six feet deep. I thoroughly enjoyed touring Honu. I've never even touched a horse before. And to get to feel him all over is a real treat. I mean, I've felt a plastic horse model before, but this one is so much more intricate. I can feel him breathing and feel his muscles twitching to shake off the flies. It's super cool!"

I knew she was smiling when she handed me a stiff bristled wooden handled brush. Putting her hand over mine, she demonstrated the direction and pressure required. She also suggested I keep one hand on his neck any time I was close to him. "That way if he moves toward you, you'll feel his weight shifting and you can back up before he steps on your foot."

"Ouch," I mumbled as I passed the brush down his soft neck. "Hey, doesn't *honu* mean turtle in Hawaiian?"

"It does."

"Is that an indication that my designated mount is slow? Because I like to go fast."

She replied, "You won't want to go fast today. Better start with a walk. We'll work you up to trotting and cantering later because tomorrow you are going to feel some muscles that today you don't know you have."

I scoffed. "Baby, every muscle in my body is honed to perfection."

"Yeah," she replied in the cool, dry tone I had come to expect from her. "We'll see."

After a demonstration of the parts of the saddle, we were ready to mount.

Everly seemed perplexed at how to teach me to get on the horse. Apparently, even a lightweight inexperienced

213

person could practically pull the animal off its feet. She told me that I would put my left foot into the stirrup—not too far in, only to the ball of the foot—and then bounce upward.

And I wasn't supposed to hold the cantle—the ridge-like thing on the back of the seat. I was supposed to grasp the saddle horn—the thing in the front shaped like a mushroom. That way, when I threw my right leg over, I wouldn't have to simultaneously move my right hand.

This was beginning to sound complicated.

"Here," she resolved. "You stand behind me when I get on. Put your hands on my hips so you can feel the motion."

It was my turn to say, "Hm." Maybe this wasn't so bad after all.

With my hands on her hips, I felt and heard her get on the horse. "This does not seem complicated," I observed.

"It isn't. But some people try to pull the horse down rather than pop themselves up. I want you to do this correctly, but I didn't know how to show you any other way."

The next issue was whether or not I could hold the reins along with the mane with my left hand while I mounted, or if I should steady the stirrup and insert my foot—but only as far as the ball of my foot—while she held the horse for me. In the end, we worked it all out. She made me mount and dismount ten times until she was certain I had the knack.

When we were finally on our way, we stopped twice while Everly opened and closed a gate. At a windmill, we let the horses get a drink. While we sat listening to the water trickle into the tank, I started thinking about the three cups of coffee I'd had after dessert.

"Uh, Everly," I began, "I don't suppose there's a Porta Pot handy, is there?"

She snorted. "There's a hundred sixty acres of bathroom in this particular pasture. Unless you need cheerleaders around."

"Not necessary," I muttered.

She said, "I can't ride away or Honu will get nervous and want to follow me. So I will leave my horse here while I go over the hill and check the grass."

"Check the grass?" I asked dubiously. "You can't just see the grass and tell how it's getting along?"

"You check the grass here. I'll check the grass over there."

"Oh. Gotcha," I replied with understanding.

When we were once again mounted, I asked how things were going with her grandpa.

She didn't answer for a while. Finally, she said, "My uncle is coming back. He's a missionary."

"Where?" I probed.

"Caribbean Islands. But he wants to come home and take over the operation."

"Did you tell your grandpa that you have vested a lot of your time and effort into the ranch?"

"Yeah." Again, there was a long silence. "But my uncle is first generation. And a male."

"So?" I prompted.

Her voice was quiet when she answered, "We'll see."

Over coffee the next morning, I confessed that I had indeed located a couple of previously undetected muscles. But overall, I told her, I had enjoyed the riding.

To my surprise and delight, she did not say I-told-you-so.

While the radio on top of the refrigerator delivered the morning news to my right ear, my phone read a deposition in my left ear. After listening to one passage twice, I engaged the display on the phone and held it up. "Everly, can you tell me what that says? It's garbled."

From across the kitchen, she said, "Good grief, that's tiny. Hang on." Setting down some utensil, she padded across the floor and leaned toward the phone. "Hold it still," she muttered as she grasped the hand with which I was holding the device.

"Here, let me see it. I have to make it bigger. The print on this thing is as tiny as the screen reader is fast."

"Are you far-sighted?" I asked.

"Yes." She mumbled the words of the deposition for a few seconds. Then she read, "I don't recall the exact time of day, but it was late. Real late."

I snorted. "Leave it to a teacher to use an adjective when she should use an adverb."

Resuming her previous work, Everly asked, "What's the case about?"

"Dolores Stoltz, a high school science teacher, came into my office a few weeks before the end of the spring term. She said her team leader had behaved in a manner she thought might be inappropriate. Shortly after that, she claimed that he had raped her. Mind you, there had been no further contact between them. She just went from maybe-it-was-inappropriate to he-raped-me."

She snorted. "Sounds like she needs a good spanking."

"Maybe that's what he offered," I shrugged.

At the next Sunday dinner (lunch) when Everly mentioned the riding, Gunnar bristled. "Everly! You're supposed to be taking care of him. Why in the hell would you put a world class athlete on a horse?"

"Some world class athletes use a horse in their sport," Everly plied.

"He's not one of them," Gunnar parried. "He'll get bucked off or get his foot stepped on."

"I put him on Honu," she said defensively.

216

Gunnar went on as though he hadn't heard her. "Besides, what good does it do him to ride a horse? He can't see where he's going anyway."

"Actually," I broke in—partly to remind them I was still here, "that's the nice part. The horse won't step off a cliff. I might."

"Stay off horses," Gunnar stated. Then, his voice a little softer, he added, "Please. What else have you been having him do?"

"I was planning to build some fence this week," she said carefully.

He pondered a moment. "I suppose tamping fence posts won't hurt him. Might make his arms and shoulders sore for a few days. Put a few blisters on his hands."

"I already have the posts set," she said.

Gunnar exploded. *"Barbed wire?* Good god, Everly! Barbed wire is dangerous even if you can see it! There are a thousand ways to kill or maim yourself when you work with barbed wire. Absolutely not! I don't want Mike within a hundred miles of a roll of barbed wire. Are we clear?"

"Crystal," she replied, sounding repentant.

He continued fuming. "My god, Ev. Barbed wire. . . What if he kneels on a barb and gets a joint infection in his knee? Or loses a finger when the tension hits a roll. Good grief. . . And fence pliers. My god. There are at least twenty-six ways to wreck your hands with fence pliers. Those damned things were invented by some kind of medieval torture specialist."

"Do you mind if I have him help work cattle?" Everly asked mildly.

Again, Gunnar erupted. "Everly! A cow steps on his foot? He gets kicked in the leg? He gets knocked into a fence? How many other ways can you think of to maim him? He's a *runner*, for Christ's sake!"

217

Still using the same even tone, she set her glass on the table and said, "I was thinking of having him sit next to the chute and input data into the computer."

There was a brief silence. Then Gunnar grunted, "Well, I suppose that can't hurt him. And it is always nice to have at least one person chuteside whose hands aren't slathered in cow shit."

Slathered? My brows drooped as a grimace slipped across my face.

The following day dawned bright and absolutely—and unusually—calm. Derek and I finished by eleven. Back at Everly's, I did my stretches and floor workout. Everly rushed in through the back door, ordered me to get changed, and handed me a sandwich on our way out the door.

As we strode toward her pickup—which was still running—she explained that the cattle were in the sorting pens and that she had left her grandparents sorting.

I didn't ask what kind of sorting they were doing. But I found out soon enough. They were separating the cows into one pen (enclosure) and their babies into another. Apparently neither bovine set appreciated this imposition. I previously had no idea that a cow could moo at over a hundred decibels. Listening to a couple hundred pairs of them simultaneously bellowing was unbelievable.

I was introduced to Grandma and Grandpa, hands were shaken all around, and my hands subsequently would not smell right for a couple days afterward despite numerous hand-washings. The afternoon's procedures would begin as soon as the vet arrived. Apparently poking fun at the vet's tardiness was a popular local pastime.

"Mike, would you like to know how this process works?" Grandpa asked.

"Sure," I replied.

He led me to the side of the chute and explained how the animal entered the back, stood inside with its neck in the headgate, and then exited through the headgate.

"Shouldn't it be called a neck-gate?" I posed.

Grandpa chuckled. Then he took my hands and put them on the side doors. There were three separate panels on the top half of each side of the ten-foot long box-like contraption. Made of a trio of what seemed like jail bars, each one opened independently to allow access to the front third, middle third, or rear third of the creature, depending what procedure was being conducted. I asked for an example of each.

"Vaccinations in the neck," he explained, "physical exam in the middle, preg checking or tail bleeding in the back."

"I was with you through the physical exam part," I observed.

"It'll make more sense as we go. Now, up here," he led me to the front and put my hands on two vertical, almost parallel pipes that were nearly five foot tall and shaped like parentheses. "This is the headgate. This is what happens when I move the lever over here."

As the lever screeched upward, the pipes spread apart.

"And when I move the lever back."

The pipes closed again.

"So the cow's neck is between the pipes?" I asked. He agreed. I added, "And assuming his head is bigger than his neck, and his shoulders are bigger than his neck, he's stuck when you close this the way it is now. Right?"

"Right. Except a cow ain't a he. A cow is a she-critter. Now, if we get a real calm cow in here, I'll let you feel around. But the youngsters—the calves—will act crazy. They would bust your hand soon as look at you."

I nodded appreciatively and pondered playing the piano with a cast on my arm.

When the vet pulled in twenty minutes late, he began hurriedly unloading armloads of equipment. "Young man," he called to me, "why don't you give me a hand?"

"I'll help you, Doc," Everly said. "This is Mike Sands from the big city, and he tends to trip and fall while carrying things."

The vet stopped in his tracks. After a moment of scrutiny, he said, "I see." Then he chuckled at his own pun and resumed his trek.

It took almost fifteen minutes for the vet to set up. My position was in a lawn chair adjacent to the side of the chute where the vet would be working.

He turned to me. "Mike, you ready?"

"Sure," I replied.

"What parameters are you logging?" he pelted.

He reminded me of Dad. Dad loves checklists. "Cow weight, hip height, pregnancy status, calf weight, vaccines, branding, and some other stuff."

Doc laughed. "Right. Bring on the beef!"

I almost jumped sideways off the chair when the first cow hit the back gate of the chute. There was a lot of clanking and clanging. And insanely loud bellowing.

A lever screeched. Doc entered the back of the chute and a moment later called, "Pregnant."

I entered *P* in the first column. "Weight?" I asked.

"Wait for what?" Doc asked as he stepped out.

From the other side of the chute, Everly yelled, "Twelve twenty-four. When you're ready for her weight, Mike, ask for 'scale' so people don't get confused."

"Okay," I mumbled as I recorded the weight. Then I raised my chin and said, "Holy cow, that's a lot of beef!"

"Sixty-two percent of her is beef," Doc offered. "The rest is hide and hooves and blood and bones and guts."

My lip wrinkled in distaste. I wondered fleetingly if I'd ever want to eat beef again.

"Hip fifty-two," Everly hollered.

"I can hear," I replied.

"Usually everything is loud when we're working cattle," she explained. "I'm not angry, and I'm not yelling at you. I just have to be loud so you'll be able to hear me."

"At least you picked a perfect day for this job," Doc pointed out. "No wind."

Just then a little whirlwind fluttered through, skittering leaves and sending a wave of dirt and grit into the air. A moment later, Everly bawled that she had sand in her eye.

"Just keep your eyes closed," I advised. "No dirt in my eyes."

"Shut up," she snapped.

Doc chuckled. "Hell, you two sound just like a married couple!"

Only once did I get off on my charting. It took Doc only a few seconds to see where I'd gone wrong and get me back on track.

"You're starting to smell pretty gamey, there, Doc," I proposed after the fiftieth cow had come and gone. "What exactly are you doing?"

"The stench is an occupational hazard," he stated. "I'm sticking my arm up her backside. At least I get to wear a long plastic glove that comes up to my armpit. Of course, I don't recall ever pregging more than ten head before the damned thing sprung a leak."

"Why don't you put on a new one every ninth cow?"

He laughed. "You want to give it a try?"

I laughed louder. "I'll leave that to the professionals. What are you looking for in there, anyway?"

"I'm not *looking* for anything. Unlike you, I do not have tiny little eyes in my fingertips, so I can't *look* for anything. But in all seriousness, I'm checking for contraband."

I nodded with grave seriousness. "Shivs. Guns. Explosives."

"Right," he belted in reply. "Cows are a rebellious lot. You can't trust them an inch."

"Just like high schoolers," I observed.

When the noise level abated at various intervals, Doc told stories that kept me in stitches. A couple times, I worried that if I didn't find a place to "check the grass," there might be an incident.

When I asked if he knew every joke on the planet, he explained that each autumn he spent six days a week standing next to a cattle chute at one ranch or another listening to the stories told by every rancher in the community.

"My second year in practice, I started writing them down. When I retire, I'm going to publish my *Compilations of Raunchy Ranch Humor*."

Compared to their mothers, the calves were indeed unruly. It took at least twice as long to get each one into the chute. It was, I was told, their very first trip through the serpentine alley that led into the chute. The youngsters were confused and scared.

Again, just like teenagers, I reflected. All bravado with their peers. Terrified when isolated and faced by authority.

When the work was nearly done on the first calf, Everly asked, "Ready?"

Doc replied through gritted teeth, "Yep."

Immediately, there followed a horrendous stench and a smoke that filled the nostrils almost like a fetid liquid. With a shriek, I abdicated my seat.

Everly laughed.

I found nothing funny in the situation. Coughing and gagging, I snapped, "That's awful!"

Doc was chuckling now. "Tell you what, Mike. Why don't we move your chair so you aren't downwind of the branding. It can be a little strong."

Even after washing my face and hands (twice), I sat at Grandma and Grandpa's table smelling like scorched hair. No one seemed to notice. The stench was ubiquitous.

It made me think of the holocaust.

It also diminished the quality of the meal that would have been otherwise exquisite.

Okay, the chocolate mousse was still impressive, even with overtones of charred hair and flesh.

On the way home, I asked Everly if the branding was actually functional or if it was some kind of cowboy heritage thing.

Instead of sounding defensive, as I expected, she explained that it is still the most definitive method to prevent theft. "We also put tattoos inside their ears and give them a plastic ear tag. Like a dangling earring. But if the tag falls out, it's hard to read the tattoo without putting them in a chute. The brand is visible from a distance."

"Theft, huh?" I thought about that for a while. "What are the cows worth?"

"The cows? Based on the current cattle market, those cows are worth about fourteen hundred bucks a head. The calves would bring about a buck eighty."

"A buck eighty?" I asked, confused.

"Per pound. Or sometimes people say they are a hundred eighty a hundredweight. That means per hundred pounds."

"Yeah, I get that. Wow. That's quite a capital investment standing out in the pasture making cowpies."

"Huge investment," she agreed. "Considering the capital investment and the low rate of return, it's a wonder anyone is involved in ranching at all."

I didn't have the nerve to ask the next question for a full minute. "Why does anyone do it?"

"It's a way of life," was her simple answer. A moment later, she elaborated. "I get to spend every day in the fresh air. As you learned today, it's not all about saddling a horse and riding into the sunset. Most of ranching is actually done with record-keeping. The more time you spend thinking and the less time you spend sweating, the more money you make. But there are plenty of hours of darkness. That's when I do the books."

"So you'll do something with all those numbers I recorded today? Or was that just to keep me busy and out of your way?" I asked glibly.

She responded with a hum.

I unbuckled my seat belt.

"How did you know we're here?" she asked as she pulled into the drive.

I scowled at her. "How would I not?"

"Because you can't see," she answered reflexively.

"Duh, Everly."

She shut off the heavy engine and pushed open her door. "It's a legitimate question," she pursued as she strode up the sidewalk to the porch.

"Not really," I observed. "I've been here a while now. Surely you've noticed that I can hear, I can smell—or at least I could before the branding— I can taste, and I can feel. You think I can't sense when you make a turn in that big overgrown sports car of a pickup truck?" Out of deference to her, until tonight, I had been calling her vehicle a pickup. Not a truck. Not a pickup truck. But I felt like goading her a bit.

Just then, as if to make her point, I missed the first step and hit the porch on my knees.

Inside, I pulled down a wineglass and filled it with water. As I sat at the kitchen table rubbing my bruised knees, I brought up the topic of barbed wire. "Sorry I can't help you with that project. But if Gunnar is so opposed, I'd better not."

She shrugged. "That's okay. He was right; it was a bad idea. I should've thought of all the things he mentioned. It can be dangerous."

"But you're going to do it anyway?"

"Have to. I'm building a new perimeter fence north of Grandpa's house. It's a five-barb fence. That means five strands."

"Sorry I can't help you," I repeated.

She sighed. "Well, you really wouldn't be much help anyway. I don't say that to be mean, Mike, but it's a visual occupation."

"I get it."

Another sigh. "You know, you're a conundrum."

"How so?" From a bottle in the refrigerator, I refilled my glass, this time with wine.

"You're so good at the things you can do. You're smart. You play the piano like no one I've ever met. You run like the wind."

I waited for the conundrum part. "But?"

She was silent.

I prompted, "But I can't sing very well."

She was still silent.

I realized she wasn't going to finish her thought. So I did it for her. "But I simply can't do simple things that simply involve seeing. Like hitting the front step with my foot instead of my knee. Like finding my phone when it's on the desk in front of me. Like folding my laundry without giving it a Braille exam first. Like pouring liquid into a cup without sticking my finger in it to determine when it's full. Like checking the weather by looking out a window."

Still silent.

I returned to my seat and took a sip. "One time I overheard my dad talking to somebody. The other guy was saying it's too bad about your kid being blind. Just think what a great runner he could've been. And Dad said, 'If Mike weren't blind, he wouldn't be a good runner.'"

Using the kindly voice she normally reserved for people other than me, Everly mused, "Dad says if you could see, you'd have been chasing skirts and drinking beer like all the other dolts out there."

I smirked. "That's right. Maybe I can teach Napili to sniff out skirts."

"He's been doing a good job running with you." Every bypassed the skirt commentary.

"You've trained him well. Maybe you should be a puppy raiser for a guide dog service," I suggested.

To my surprise, she said, "I always wanted to be a vet."

"Why didn't you go to vet school?" I begged. "I mean, why don't you go to vet school?"

"I applied. Wasn't accepted. It's easier to get into medical school than vet school. But I didn't want to go to medical school."

"So you went to work for the government," I offered, hoping she might elaborate on just what job she had done for Uncle Sam.

She didn't. Instead, she said, "Maybe Napili could become a guide dog."

"I think he's too old," I said. "Anyway, guide dog services raise puppies from certain bloodlines. And not all of the pups make the grade. A friend told me how they select candidates for training. She said they take a puppy— I think at seven weeks of age—into a strange room full of new and different objects, furnishings, and people. She sets the puppy down in the center of the room and walks away briskly.

"She said all puppies will cower for a few seconds. Then the Group A puppies will straighten up and start sniffing everything and running from object to object checking things out. The Group B puppies rise more slowly and begin to carefully and methodically check out their new environment. The Group C puppies slink toward the wall and hide under something. Guess which ones make the best guide dogs?"

"Group B," she said without hesitation. "Because they are curious, smart, and interested, but the Group A dogs are too brash."

"You are absolutely correct. Know what happens with the Group A puppies?"

She thought about it for a while, and then ventured, "They get adopted out as pets."

"They get sent to the police academy to become bomb sniffers or K-9 cops. The Group C dogs go to homes where they get to just be a dog and not have to deal with pedestrian traffic, trains, buses, elevators, and the like."

"Have you ever had a guide dog?" she asked.

"Three of them. Emma, a yellow lab, was with me until I got my first principal job. Then she retired and went to live with my aunt and uncle in Fresno. Then I got Alf. He's a German shepherd. He retired two years ago after he developed some hind limb issues, and he is now in a home with a young family in nearby Sacramento. I still have visitation rights." I grinned. "Then I got Harley."

"He's the one who died suddenly?" she asked.

The question stopped me for a second. "Didn't you just ask me a minute ago if I'd ever had a guide dog?"

"I did. But after I asked, I remembered you told me about the one who died a few months ago," she said.

I lay awake that night considering her question. For some reason, it made me uneasy. But I had no idea why.

Except that I did know why.

I had never mentioned Harley—or his untimely death—to Everly. I was certain of it.

In the middle of the night, I woke sitting up, rubbing my eyes, a habit my mother had badgered out of me by the age of six. Later on, when Mom couldn't see me in the college dorm, I had begun to allow myself the soothing ten-second rub before bed. But tonight, this was deep, hard pressing.

Everly was suddenly standing in the doorway. "What are you doing? Quit that."

"Why does it bother you?" I snapped, only partially awake.

"Why do you do it?" she asked calmly.

I thought about that. Why was I doing it? Why was I even awake? I was sure I had been sleeping. A quick check of my watch revealed that it was past eleven. I had gone to bed two hours earlier. Certainly, I must have been asleep.

Suddenly I snapped my face toward her. "Everly, I think I'm losing my mind."

"Are you awake?" she appealed as she leaned against the doorframe.

Dropping my hands, I asked, "What do I smell? What is that?"

She sniffed. Then she stepped inside the room, still testing the air.

I asked, "Don't you ever sleep?"

"Sure. What smell? All I can smell is your laundry."

"Yeah. What is that? It's the smell of branding. The burning hair." I shuddered. "Everly, I'm losing my mind."

She waited a moment and finally asked, "What are you talking about?"

"I smelled that smell once before. On the jet. Right before it crashed. I smelled burning hair. But only for a few seconds. Is that nuts? Am I going crazy?"

"When you first woke up on the plane, you mean?"

"Yeah." After I replied, I wondered how she knew I had been sleeping on the flight.

Something was not right in my world. And Everly Galloway seemed to be in the middle of everything that was not right.

Chapter Nine

With another race on the schedule in five weeks, a carefully planned list of daily workouts, and multiple assurances that I would call at least once a day to report on my workout progress, I entrusted Derek's birthday gift to Shelley to hold for three days. Then I tossed my suitcase into the bed of Everly's pickup and climbed into the passenger seat, ready for the trip to California.

It seemed funny to be going back. On one hand, I felt like I was going home. On the other, I felt like I was leaving home.

The route was easy enough. Twenty miles south of town, we picked up Interstate 80 and pointed west toward Solomon, California. I was glad Everly liked to drive. I slept a lot of the way.

In eastern Nevada, I climbed onto a hotel treadmill and ran for an hour while Everly lounged in the hot tub and pool across the glass wall. It was one of those times I longed to not be blind. I really would have enjoyed watching her frolic in her swimsuit.

The next morning, she asked how anyone could sleep for ten hours in a pickup and then sleep seven hours on a bed. I put in four miles on the treadmill, ate enough breakfast for three people at the buffet included in the price of the hotel, and returned to the passenger seat in her pickup.

It was mid-afternoon when we got to town. According to Mom's most recent text, she was still playing cards with her bridge club, and Dad was at work. So we drove to the school district offices. Nina Marbury was behind her desk.

She jumped up and gave me a hug and said how sorry she was for me to go. I scowled and said, "You won't miss telling me where my coffee cup is."

She laughed. "Yes, actually, I will. And I still miss Harley, poor boy."

"Nina, this is Everly Galloway. She's my bodyguard." I managed to keep a straight face. For a few seconds. Then I grinned. "She's also teaching me to drive a ranch pickup and ride horses."

"Oh, my!" Nina said as she shook hands with Everly. "Sounds like you have your work cut out for you."

Nina had packed my personal items into a couple of big boxes. I hadn't realized I'd accumulated so much stuff. And I was glad I didn't have to tote them home with one hand while white-caning with the other. Both boxes would easily fit in the back of Everly's truck. Pickup.

On the way out of the building, we were stopped by a voice from behind. "*Mister* Sands! As I live and breathe! You came home!"

I turned and set down the box I was carrying. "Hey, JJ! How are you?"

"I'm good," he said as he took my hand. "I'm helping out here at the school for the summer. But what do I hear about you leaving us? Are you really gonna go win the Olympics?"

"Sure," I said as I shook his hand. "Unless the other guys run faster than I do. How's school going?"

"It's going great. I already got a job lined up for when I graduate next year. First person ever in my family to go to college! My mama's got a big party planned and all that. And I got you to thank for it. I never woulda done it without you convincing me I could."

"Hey, you can thank me when I start writing your term papers and taking your finals," I scolded. "Until then, it's all you. And I never doubted for a minute that you would graduate. Good luck, JJ."

When we were buckled in Everly's pickup, she put the truck in gear and said, "How many people have you pushed into college who wouldn't have made it otherwise?"

I smiled. "Pushed? Maybe influenced. Helped. Assisted. I'll never know. I hope a lot. It's only three blocks to my place. Turn left at the stop sign."

"I guess it's good to live close since you have to walk to work."

"It's very good. It's a tiny house, but that means it's easy to clean. And with no cars to junk it up, the two-car garage makes a great space for the treadmill and gym and piano. When the weather is nice, which is most of the time here, I can open the big doors when I run."

I slipped the key into the lock and talked myself out of goose bumps that threatened to form on the back of my neck. I had been in the house since the gunman had been killed, and Rosalee Kazemi's body had been dumped.

But I hadn't slept here overnight.

We dropped off the boxes and drove to my folks' house. Mom had just gotten home.

I introduced her to Everly. They seemed to hit it off which, to my slight surprise, left me feeling relieved.

When we were seated at the table, each of us with a tall glass of iced tea, Everly asked, "Mrs. Sands, Mike told me you found out he was blind when he was six months old. What was that like for you?"

232

This story would be a rerun for me. I was about to get up and go play the piano. But Mom's words riveted me to the slick, polished wooden chair.

"Six months? I knew there was something wrong with him in the first twenty-four hours. One of the things I had really enjoyed with my first child was that magical time when I was breastfeeding, and we just looked into each other's eyes. But right away, I noticed Mike didn't look at me. My first stupid thought was that he didn't like me. But that fear was quickly replaced by the prospect that he might be autistic.

"When I took him in for his two-week checkup, the doctor looked him all over and pronounced that he was perfect. She asked if I had any questions. I choked. Who was I to disagree with a professional who had just told me my baby was perfect? So I went home and pretended that everything was okay.

"Dave was deployed when Mike was born. Three months later, he came home and a few days after that, we're back at the pediatrician's office for a routine checkup. Out of the blue, he tells the doctor that the baby can't see. I was shocked! I mean, to just come right out and say it like that. How could he do that? He hadn't said anything to me about it.

"But the doctor said it was easy enough to test. She took Mike down the hall and ten minutes later came back and told us our baby had no light perception. She made us an appointment with the ophthalmologist in the same complex. We saw him three weeks later and got the same news. He sent us to a world renowned pediatric eye specialist who, fortunately for us, was just down the road in San Francisco.

"In the five weeks between first being told he couldn't see and going to that final ophtho visit, I cried and cried. Then, after we left the specialist's office, neither of us spoke for a good half hour. Finally David said, 'When he told us this baby is blind, he gave us the good news and the bad news. The bad news is that he'll never see. But the good news is that's the whole story. Unlike some babies with this diagnosis, his kidneys are fine. His lungs are fine. His brain is fine. And do you know what impressed me the most? He told us he hoped we could find someone to prove him wrong.'"

Mom took a deep breath. I reached across the table and found her hand.

She squeezed my hand in response. "Dave told me it was time to stop grieving—though he never shed a tear that I know of—and start figuring out how to successfully raise a blind kid. So we made that our focus."

"I had no idea," I mumbled.

Turning from Everly to me, Mom said, "I never told you this because I never wanted you to feel like you were responsible for your blindness or for the ramifications it had on our family. We didn't want to raise you to be a blind person. We wanted to raise you to be a decent, productive member of society who happened to be blind."

Before I could respond to that, Everly asked, "So you never really got a medical diagnosis to explain why he's blind?" She had asked me the same question. And I had relayed to her the same spiel I'd given a hundred times before: Nobody knows.

"Oh, sure." My mother rattled off the foreign-sounding title with ease, leaving me to wonder why I'd never heard it before.

Squeezing her hand again, I whispered, "Love you, Mom."

Mom squeezed my hand in return and, turning to Everly, said wryly, "We knew right away there was nothing wrong with his voice. Once he started talking, he never quit. Even talks in his sleep."

When my tea glass was empty, I left the women at the table and went into the living room.

Despite internet reports, I couldn't square the Charles I knew with a high level terrorist. So I mouthed a text into my phone. "Charles, this is Mike Sands. Period. Again, comma, I wish to extend my deepest condolences to you and your family. Period." I then repeated the diagnosis for my blindness, in case he was interested, apologized for not knowing how to spell it, and wished him well.

In less than a minute, Charles rang me. He began with a heartfelt apology for the text that had come from his phone but which he purported not to have seen until my new message arrived.

"I assumed someone else sent it," I responded. Given his impeccable vocabulary and formal command of the language, I knew Charles could have penned a vicious missive had he wanted to. ROT IN HELL YOU F-ING PIG hardly seemed eloquent.

Besides, he would have used correct punctuation.

"Mike, I can assure you that your assumption is correct. I did not see the vile message until just now when your latest text came through." Then he changed the subject abruptly. "Tell me, please, who diagnosed your ophthalmologic condition."

After my very brief recitation of the facts, he said he knew the exact identity of the unnamed San Francisco doctor. And he added that if that man had made the determination, he did not doubt its veracity. "My friend, when will you be visiting in California again? We should meet for coffee. There is a project I wish to discuss with you."

"Coffee? Not a run?" I inquired.

"Ah, at your suggestion, I have been to the body shop and am now the proud owner of a newly replaced knee. It has been two weeks since the surgical procedure, and I believe the physical therapists would frown upon the suggestion of a five-mile run. Alas," he added dryly, "merely to consider such an endeavor at this moment causes me to wince, I am afraid."

Even if Charles harbored ill will toward me, which I doubted, I suspected he would not try to harm me at a public coffee house, so I made arrangements to meet him during my visit.

Dad came home an hour later. Feeling light and jubilant, I shook his hand and said, "Dad, I'd like you to meet Everly Galloway. Everly, this is my dad, David."

He greeted her with, "How are you, Special Agent Galloway?"

And she said, "Nice to see you again, Colonel."

Something inside me went empty. Vacuous.

But suddenly a lot of things fell into place. Suddenly, I knew how Dad had known I smelled dog poop before the doomed flight. Suddenly, I knew how Everly knew my guide dog had died inexplicably and how she had known I was sleeping before the plane crashed.

I said little during supper (dinner) and was quiet on the way to my house afterward. When Mom had asked me a week ago where Everly would stay during our visit, I had suggested she could sleep in the spare bed at my place. To Mom, I had said I would feel more secure knowing someone else was in the house—someone who could see strangers lurking in the kitchen.

But really I had been thinking that once I got Everly away from the ranch and the cows, I might have a chance of lighting a few fireworks with her.

Riding toward my house in her truck now, I felt no inclination toward fireworks. Not with her. Not with the woman who had never mentioned that she knew my dad— and on a professional, not personal, basis.

"Is the altitude getting to you?" she quipped. "There is a lot of sighing coming from over there."

After a while, I replied, "My ego took a pretty hard hit tonight. You'll have to give me time to adjust." I would have added, "But don't worry about me. I can fall in love again someday. As soon as I find a woman who is young and naïve enough to put up with a handicapped husband."

But somehow, I thought the statement might give her some satisfaction. And I was too stingy for that.

"Mike," she began slowly, "perhaps I should have told you about the arrangement."

"The arrangement? The arrangement with my dad, you mean? The arrangement where he hired you to babysit me?"

She said nothing.

Nor did I.

She did comment, however, when we walked inside. "Why do you keep the piano in the garage?"

"Better acoustics."

"Are you planning to run now?" she asked.

"Yes."

I turned away from her and went to my room to find some running clothes. When I came out, she said, "I'm ready. Where's the tether?"

"The treadmill is in the garage. Right beside the grand piano. Excuse me."

I tried to pass her, but she stood in my way. She said, "I'm ready to run. Let's go."

I made no reply.

"Come on," she pleaded, "show me your neighborhood."

Figuring she could only last for a couple miles at best, I shrugged and grabbed a bungee cord from the wall next to the door.

We ran the first mile at seven-minute pace. Then we kicked it up to six-minute.

To my downright surprise, she ran ten miles at that pace. I wanted to ask why she hadn't told me she was a runner. But apparently there were a lot of things she hadn't told me. I wasn't sure I could stand to learn any more of them today.

The rest of the week, I managed to spend most of my time away from Everly, though she did drive me to the district attorneys' offices on Wednesday for the Stoltz case management conference and to the courthouse on Thursday where I testified as an expert witness in another case. I wasn't sure, but I thought she stayed in the courtroom the whole time.

It must have been exciting for her. All that procedural posturing. Dry as old paint.

Though the court had scheduled me to testify on Thursday and Friday, I was released on Thursday an hour past lunch. They wouldn't need me the following day.

I had decided not to talk to Everly any more than was necessary, but as we left the courthouse, I did ask, "Did you see anybody there pointing a gun at me?"

"Not today," she replied. "Were you expecting anyone to be?"

My answer was a shrug.

The following morning, I left the house stealthily and, without bodyguard, met Charles at a café. We had a delightful visit and, as always, I departed from him feeling wiser.

Despite my own personal disappointment over my relationship (or lack thereof) with Everly, I enjoyed the anniversary party on Saturday afternoon. Afterward, Dad treated us kids and our spouses (or in my case bodyguard) and my nieces and nephews to dinner at a nice steak house. I was told it was also an early birthday celebration for me.

The following morning, everyone had breakfast at Mom and Dad's. Then, after packing everything I thought I would need in Nebraska for the next several months, I climbed into Everly's truck for the eastbound trip.

It was a quiet trip.

Bypassing the historical places we had previously discussed visiting on our return, we drove straight through to Wyoming the first day. When we walked into the lobby of the hotel, I asked for a room with two beds. The very polite clerk told me the price, told me where to find the pool and the breakfast room, and offered a sheet of paper listing local eateries.

"You can give that to my Man Friday," I said, nodding toward Everly.

Jovially, he said, "You look more like a Girl Friday to me."

She wordlessly took the paper.

A moment later, he handed me a room key. As I took hold of it, he directed, "Sir, feel the edges of the card."

I did. On the edge of one short side there was a semicircular notch chipped out of the hard plastic.

"If you hold the card so that the notch is on the right side of the edge closest to you, the card is in position to unlock the door."

Despite my sour mood, I smiled. "Thank you. Usually I have to slide the card in four times before I get it right."

Returning the smile, he said, "My aunt was born blind. She told me she had that problem, too. So I devised this method to help her out."

"Very clever," I remarked. "You should pass this along to the management of this chain."

He said, "I would, but we're in the process of switching all the locks to the kind where you just tap the card against the lock. It doesn't matter which direction you hold them."

Holding up the key card, I thanked him again.

After I returned to the hotel room from my very long and boring treadmill run, I took a shower and pulled on better smelling running shorts and a clean t-shirt.

As I emerged from the bathroom, I heard Dad's voice on Everly's phone. She said, "He's here now, Colonel. Go ahead."

"Am I on speaker so you can both hear me?" he asked.

"You are," she verified.

"Yeah," I grumbled.

"Mike, Everly, I am calling to extend my deepest apologies. Mike, I didn't tell you about my business relationship with Everly because I didn't want to concern you. I have eight of my best people—including myself and Everly—investigating your case. But it never occurred to me that you two might develop feelings for each other. As usual, your mother picked up on the emotional aspect of this. And as usual, I missed it. I didn't realize until you left—and your mother threatened to hit me over the head with a brick— that I had caused any problems between you two. So kiss and make up."

Without further ado, he disconnected.

Neither of us spoke for a full minute.

Then I said, "Does that page the hotel clerk handed you show a good steakhouse near here?"

She slid the paper from the table between the beds. Within seconds, she relayed, "There's one in walking distance."

I said, "Let's go."

When we left the steakhouse to return to the hotel, I had my hand lightly on her arm just above her elbow. As we walked, I let it slide down until we were walking hand in hand. It's not as safe to walk that way, but I trusted her not to run me off the path.

In the hallway approaching our room, she asked, "Does a Braille number two look like a backwards L?"

"No. The L-looking thing is a numeral character. It tells you that the next character is a number, not a letter. After the backward L, an A becomes a 1. B is a 2, and so on."

"Oh," she said. "I see. So every room on this floor starts with a B."

I grinned. "Something like that. Hotels are the easiest places to get around. They are good about Braille signs next to every door. They don't always proofread the signs, but they usually have them."

"What do you mean about the proofreading?" she probed.

"I've found signs that say *Baundry* or *Thorage* or *Staff Obly*."

She put my hand on a plaque next to our room door.

I read the Braille. "Two-oh-four."

"Good," she said. "I got the right room."

She slid the card key into the slot and pushed the door open. I followed her inside. She swiftly crossed to the far wall and then returned.

"Any boogie men slinking around on the floor between the beds?" I asked.

"All clear," she replied.

"Good."

Standing now just in front of me, she asked, "Which bed do you want?"

"Yours." I cupped her cheeks in my hands and kissed her.

When I was in high school, my sister had invited a bunch of her buddies over to watch a movie. One of the girls had commented that she thought it was so romantic when a man caressed a woman's cheek before he kissed her.

For me, it was less a matter of romance and more a desire not to kiss her eyebrow or break her nose.

241

For the first second or two, Everly did not respond. Then she slipped her hands to my back.

I wrapped my arms around her and drew her close.

But something came between us. Leaning backward, I indicated the gun at her waist and said, "You're still working."

She pulled away from me. I thought she would unbuckle her belt and toss the holster and gun on the bed. Instead, she said softly, "You're right. I am still working. And until I'm sure you're out of danger, I will stay on the job."

I dropped my chin to my chest. After taking a deep breath and letting it out to vent my frustration, I said, "I want a male bodyguard."

"Why?"

From her tone, I knew I had struck a nerve. And it wasn't the one at which I'd been aiming. "Not because I don't think you're competent. But because I don't like being attracted to my bodyguard."

"Well, I'm sorry. But romantic entanglement isn't professional."

"Are you working for my dad or for the FBI?" I inquired.

She didn't answer.

I repeated the question.

She repeated the silence.

As I dropped onto the bed, I emitted the same guttural sound I'd made upon learning about high, thin overcast. After lying there for a half hour with my hands clasped behind my head, I asked, "Have you ever been whitewater rafting?"

She replied that she'd had a chance once, but work had prevented her making the trip, so her friends had gone without her.

I sent a quick text to Paul Stuebbens and got an almost immediate reply. Sure, the cabin was available. He sent the code that would get us in the side door and bid us a great time. And, he added, definitely don't miss out on the rafting. Best time of the year for it.

After a few wrong turns, we found the cabin. We dropped off our luggage and then drove back up the road a half mile to a restaurant we'd passed. Bantering with the waitress, I inquired into local whitewater rafting companies. She said only one had survived the shootings.

"Shootings?" I bit.

"Oh, surely you heard about it," she began with relish. "It was the biggest news in the state for a while. Some nut holed up in the rocks along the river and took random shots at rafters. Of course, they caught the guy, but not until three of the four local rafting companies went belly up."

Armed with a phone number, we called and reserved a trip for the following day.

Our guide explained to seven passengers the safety rules and, owing to the fact that he had taken blind rafters down the river before, gave me some extra tips. Then he asked me, "Do you ever get motion sickness in a boat?"

"Never have," I answered.

"That's what I figured. People look at the water and lose their equilibrium. But you won't have that problem."

He also reminded us that the temperature of the water— water which had only recently resided on a mountaintop in the form of snow—was barely above freezing.

Fifteen minutes after we left the dock, we found out how right he was about the water temperature.

The first inkling I had that the trip was not progressing as expected was when our guide gave a very unusual-sounding grunt and slumped over in my lap.

Things happened fast after that. So fast that I don't know exactly how I ended up in the water except to say that the raft seemed to dissolve from under me.

Like a rag doll, I was slammed from rock to rock. First a shoulder blade. Then a thigh. Then an ankle.

From my dad, I had learned that the most common cause of water-related deaths was panic.

Ninety percent of my concentration was subsumed in fighting panic. The other half was spent trying to stay upright with my head in the air and feet in the water and not vice versa.

Did I mention that the water was cold? Frigid!

My fingers and feet were quickly becoming numb. Then my left shoulder slammed against the edge of a rock, sending shock waves down the arm.

I grasped at a rock. Lost my grip. Slipped back into the water.

Finally, after what felt like ages, I managed to wedge my right wrist between two rocks. I pushed my right foot against something that felt solid, but the tread of my soaked running shoe slipped and nearly sent me back into the current.

With a second feeble attempt, I managed to get my left arm over a big flat, nearly vertical rock. Hugging the rock for all I was worth, I leaned against it, spluttering, gasping.

There was a voice somewhere above and behind me. "Mike! Go to your right! Go right! You're almost out of the river."

Again, I shoved my foot against a rock. Again, it slipped. Finally on the third try, I succeeded in launching myself to the right.

I landed on another flat rock, this one nearly horizontal. My feet were still in water, but the rest of me was in the sunshine.

I couldn't move. All I could do was pant and cough.

"Mike, I can't get to you." I recognized the voice as one of our raft-mates. Penny Somebody. She and her daughter had been sitting to my left. I couldn't remember the daughter's name. No matter. Penny called over the swift rushing water, "Mike, you'll have to get up here on your own. My arm's broken. Go straight forward for two feet. Then you'll have to climb up the bank. I'll give you directions."

Very slowly, I pushed myself to hands and knees. My feet were numb.

I tried to speak. Cleared my throat. Tried again. "Penny, where is Everly?"

"I don't know. Can you stand up?"

Straining to hear any other voices over the rushing water, I called, "How far did we go? I mean, how long was I in the water?"

She thought about it a moment, and then replied, "I think about a hundred yards. About a football field."

Football fields are flat. With soft grass, I thought. Not a pile of rocks with a fire hose torrent of water bashing around between them.

"Can you walk?" she called.

I got to my feet. Numb feet. Freezing feet.

But, I reminded myself, feet that could run forty miles in a day. Magic feet. Special feet.

I took a careful step, put down my frozen magic foot. Took another step.

So far, so good.

It was the fourth step when I slipped.

The next time I was aware, there was someone hovering over me. In the distance, I could hear Penny's voice. "He's blind. . . I mean totally blind. He can't see you."

Penny's voice sounded strained now, undoubtedly due to her broken arm.

"His girlfriend was with him. Or maybe his wife, I don't know. I can't see her. I don't know where she is."

"Where's Everly?" I croaked.

The man hovering over me said, "We'll figure that out in a little while. Right now, we need to get you up on the road so we can check you over. Can you see me?"

"I'm blind," I answered. My voice sounded odd. Probably from gargling the river.

"Like, totally blind?"

"Like totally blind," I answered. "Since birth. My eyes don't point the same direction, and they don't respond to light."

"Okay. That's good to know." He sounded relieved. "Otherwise, we were gonna take you in for brain surgery. Can you move your feet?"

I moved my feet. I think. They were still frozen.

"How about your hands?"

Ditto.

"All right," he said. "Looks like you're gonna need a few stitches in your head."

I groaned. "I made it out of the lousy river. Then I tripped on a rock."

"Your lucky day," he agreed.

I was in the hospital at least an hour before anyone told me anything about Everly.

Drifting in and out of a semi-sickly sleep, I realized someone was holding my hand. "Everly?" I mumbled.

"I'm right here. You're gonna be fine," she said softly.

I sighed. "Are you okay?"

"Yes. I barely even got wet. I practically stepped from the raft onto a rock. But when I grabbed for you, I missed."

I squeezed her hand.

We didn't leave the hospital for four hours. That's how long it took the cops to question me about whether or not I

246

might have been the target of the sniper who shot and killed our guide and simultaneously deflated the raft.

Dead dog. Plane crash. Unidentified home invader. Dead body in the spare bedroom. Sexual harassment suits. And now raft shooters.

When I was finally allowed to go despite the emergency room physician waffling over whether I should stay overnight, I whispered to Everly, "Let me put my arm over your shoulder when we walk out of here. Blind people—deaf people, for that matter—are more likely to tumble if we are a little light-headed. Fewer cues to give us our position in space."

"Gotcha," she replied softly. "I've got your back."

"I'll get your front," I offered.

She scoffed. "Watch it or you might have a new reason to spend the night here after all."

From a hotel bed, I called Dad and admitted, "I think you might be onto something."

Chapter Ten
⠨⠀⠄ ⠏⠂⠩ ⠀⠲⠏⠐⠒

The trip back to Nebraska, though not long in miles, was long in pain. I felt like. . . well, I felt like I'd been battered against rocks. Derek came over in the afternoon to see if I wanted to go for a short run. I did. He asked to see my back. I slowly and gingerly peeled off my t-shirt. He made appreciative noises and suggested we take the day off. So we only ran four miles.

The following morning, Napili accompanied us. We were a mile into our run, working out the kinks, when Derek said, "You remember how I told you I admire you for being upbeat all the time? The other night I was lying in bed thinking about what it must be like. I was remembering that Sunday dinner the first week you were here. We asked you about blindness, and you told a funny story. Asked you about insensitive comments, and you told a funny story. Asked you about anything, and you told a funny story."

I waited to see if he planned to end his comments with a question mark. Apparently, he didn't. After a while, I told him about my great-aunt's advice that I had better find a wife who was young and naïve.

"Your great-aunt sounds like a battle ax," he noted.

"Maybe," I said. "But as I've gotten older, girlfriends have gotten scarcer."

He quipped, "You don't suppose that holding down a full time job and a full time training schedule keeps you out of the dating game, do you?"

"Nope. I'm sure that has nothing to do with it," I replied lightly.

"But you and Everly are a couple, right?"

I didn't answer for four strides. Then, trying to keep my voice as free of emotion as possible, I stated, "Everly and I are not a couple."

"Since when? I thought you two were an item long ago."

Instead of addressing that issue, I told him about a girl I'd dated in college. "On the one-year anniversary of our first date, I proposed to her. She was aghast. No way would she ever marry a blind man. She just liked being the girl who was going out with him. Just as my great-aunt predicted, that girl had no intention of being saddled to a cripple for life."

Then I told him about the physical education requirement at college and how I had gone to speak with the head of the department to see if he had recommendations for the best classes for me to take. "The university offered over a hundred twenty PE courses," I said. "But he wanted to waive the requirement for me. I said I didn't want the requirement waived. I wanted to know which course he thought would be better. He was adamant. Didn't want me to get hurt and sue the school."

"What did you do?" Derek probed.

"As I was leaving his office, I ran into a sweet, little old lady—and I mean I literally ran into her. She introduced herself as Dr. Seltzer, took me into her office, and asked me to sign up for Social Dance 110. I asked her what the course entailed and why she particularly wanted me to take it. She outlined the dance steps I would learn and lamented that she never had enough men signed up. Because of the imbalance, the female students in her classes frequently ended up dancing with other girls. She said it worked out okay because many of them were dance majors who needed to learn to lead and to follow so they could teach the steps later.

"For me, the class was outstanding. I always got to dance with a girl—there were seven guys and twenty-three girls in the class. It was a rare opportunity for me to touch women without getting slapped."

Derek laughed and said, "See? You always make everything funny."

"Defense mechanism, maybe," I offered. "My fourth and fifth grade PE teacher wasn't funny. He insisted that I go out on the field and play soccer with my classmates. Soccer. Can you imagine how boring soccer is for me? So I just ran. I'd run until someone yelled to turn around. Or until I hit the fence."

Derek chortled. "You hit the fence? What kind of fence?"

"Chain link. Oh, brother. I've run into classier things than chain link fences, trust me. But for every jerk like that PE teacher, I've met a gem. Like my fifth grade teacher who announced one day that our class would be going on a field trip to an art museum."

After only a second, Derek howled. "Oh, that sounds great. Standing around staring at pictures. Perfect for a blind kid!"

"Right. So I told Mom about it, and she promised she'd excuse me from the field trip and that she and I would do something special that day—just the two of us. But when the morning of the field trip came, she told me to get ready for school. I was crestfallen. I reminded her of our deal, but she just told me to buck up and get ready to go. The only saving grace was that she said she was going on the trip as one of the parent chaperones.

"So we got to the museum, and the teacher broke our class into groups. She sent one group to one wing and another group to another wing, and so on. Then she said if anyone wanted to, they could go to the special exhibit with Mike and his mom."

I paused to breathe. Then I continued. "It was a special traveling exhibit designed especially for the visually impaired. The exhibits were connected to each other by fuzzy ropes, all the signs were in Braille, and everything was meant to be touched."

Derek started snickering.

I rebuked, "I just told you about one of the most touching experiences of my life, and you're laughing."

He said, "No, man. It's a beautiful story. But I was just imagining a Braille sign that says 'Do Not Touch'."

That sent us into a fit of giggles. And every giggle reminded me of every rock I had run into in the river.

I said, "Your turn. I'm out of breath. You talk for a while."

"Aw, nuts," Derek guffawed. "You figured me out. I just get you started yapping, and I can run and run while you huff and puff."

"Careful, or I'll cut your tether," I threatened. "Then you won't be able to breathe."

"I think you mean umbilicus, not tether," he said. When we had both recovered from laughing, he prompted, "I heard Everly telling her dad you broke your ankle one time."

I nodded and hoped he was looking. It can be challenging to hear someone nod while you're running outdoors.

He prompted, "Lost some dorso-flexion, she said."

"I think that's what you call it. I can't bend my toes up toward my shin as far on that side."

He agreed. "That's dorso-flexion."

251

I said, "I would expect a guy with a physiology degree to know that."

"My degree is in kinesiology. Not physiology. But it's all related."

After a quarter mile, Derek started snickering. Then he said, "Last night, Tish and I decided we would try sex like blind people."

I scoffed. "Did your experiment land anyone in the emergency room?"

"It was fun," he said, still cackling. "I gotta tell you, as beautiful as I think my wife is when she's pregnant, she feels even more beautiful than she looks. It was amazing."

"You're welcome," I stated.

"Which brings me to our political topic of the day," Derek announced. "Ours is a very wanted pregnancy. But what about unwanted pregnancy and—here it comes! Your favorite topic: abortion. So, what do you think? You're pro-choice, right?"

I groaned. "Let's talk about something else. I'm wounded."

"Nope. You wanted to run in the big league. So let's hear it. What are your thoughts?"

"I am pro-choice," I agreed. "I think everyone beyond the age of consent has the choice to have sex or not."

"No, come on," he urged.

"What's your stance?" I asked.

"I'm Catholic. You know what my stance is," he said.

"Not necessarily," I countered.

"Okay. I'm Catholic, and I agree with the Catholic Church on the topic of abortion. So how about you?"

I picked up the pace just a little. It didn't hurt any more to run faster than slower. "Okay. First of all, I don't think anyone ever set out with the intention of getting pregnant or getting someone pregnant for the sole purpose of having an abortion. Fair enough?"

"Probably," he said somewhat dubiously.

"Secondly, I think it is horrific to kill a fetus inside the safety of the womb. Agreed?"

"Absolutely." He liked that one.

"Thirdly, I have seen children in the school system who are loved by no one. Cared for by no one. Neglected. Despised. Used. Abused. They are in school only because the state says they have to be. They are in their homes only because they provide their parent or guardian with a government-issued paycheck so that said parent can buy drugs and liquor. They live in squalor, places where you wouldn't keep a pig. The odds against them are astronomical. They are at higher risk for suicide, chemical dependency, criminal activity, gang violence, and creating more unwanted babies. Do I think someone did those kids a favor bringing them into the world?"

"You can't be the judge and jury for everybody, man," Derek rebuked. "One of those kids might grow up to cure cancer or invent some device that will sense bombs. Hell, one of them might fix blindness so you can see a rainbow."

I didn't say anything for a while. Partly because I was out of breath after my big speech, but mostly because I didn't want to continue this conversation. "They're more likely to hand me a one dollar bill for change and tell me it's a ten."

Sounding skeptical, he said, "Why would someone do that?"

"So she could slip the other nine dollars into her pocket. So she could buy more drugs later. So she could screw over the blind guy who lives down the street. How should I know what she was thinking? I'm not a criminal; I don't understand the criminal mentality."

Derek didn't speak for a full minute. Then he said, "Did someone actually do that? Give you a one dollar bill instead of a ten?"

"Yes. Probably more than once. But one time, for sure."

Now that we were on the topic of criminal activity, he asked, "So is someone really trying to kill you?"

"If he is, he's not very good at it," I mused. "Why? Do you feel like you're in the edge of a big target sign plastered on my head?"

He sounded oddly serious. "Let's hope not. Why do you say he's not very good at it? I mean, besides the obvious fact that you're still alive."

"That's the only reason. I mean, there must be some more reliable way to kill somebody than to blow up a plane. Although, come to think of it, that seems fairly reliable. But why risk blowing up the other three hundred people on board? That's just nuts. And if you send a gunman to my house, why does he just stand there and stare at me instead of shooting me? And if you want to kill me in a raft, why not wait until I'm sitting still so you hit the right guy? If someone is trying to kill me, it must be a Keystone Cop."

Derek hadn't heard of the Keystone Cops, so I told him what I knew of them. Which wasn't much.

Back at the house after our run, I went to the kitchen for chocolate milk. Pulling the jug from the door, I popped off the lid and took a huge swig.

And then spat it into the sink. It wasn't chocolate. The jug feels the same whether its contents are luscious chocolate or blandly horrific plain milk. But the taste was definitely not the same.

When I rested my hand on the front edge of the sink, I found a slip of paper. I was moving it aside when I realized it had bumps on it. Not exactly perfect Braille, probably done with a ball point pen, it said: Meki, peano tunir comeng today. Iv.

At least I think that's what it said. Ball point stabs on paper aren't particularly accurate. And I had to interpret the reversed e's and i's.

I downed one glass of water and was in the middle of a second when I heard a knock at the front door. Presuming that a would-be murderer wouldn't knock, I crossed the living room and, through the screen door, asked, "May I help you?"

"I am Leroy. The piano tuner."

"Oh, hi," I greeted as I pulled back the door. "Come on in. Everly told me you were coming. Her F two above middle C is pretty hard to listen to."

"You the blind runner?" Leroy inquired.

"That's me," I answered as I stuck out my hand expecting a hand shake. There was none.

"Where's the piano?" he asked.

"It's right in there," I gestured, wondering why he hadn't taken my hand.

He didn't move. After a moment, he said, "Did Everly tell you anything about me?"

"She said you were coming this afternoon," I replied.

"Did she tell you I'm blind?"

I let out a self-deprecating laugh. "No, sir. She did not. And I just broke the cardinal rule of giving directions to the blind: never say it's-in-there! Shake my hand, and then come with me and hope no sighted people see us. We are truly the blind leading the blind."

Laughing at ourselves, we fumbled around until our hands connected.

I led him to the piano and asked if there was anything he needed before I returned to the kitchen.

"Play me something with that bad note," he suggested as he set down his tool kit and began rummaging in it.

"What would you like to hear?" I asked as I slid onto the bench.

"'When the Saints Go Marching In,'" he suggested.

With relish, I played a Dixieland version of the song. To my ecstatic surprise, he joined in with a voice reminiscent of Louis Armstrong. Recognizing that the song was not quite in his range, I dropped it a couple half-steps.

After several verses with various improvisational interpretations, we heard clapping from the doorway.

"Very nice!" Everly said warmly. "You guys should hire out."

"When I was a kid, I wanted to be a famous musician," Leroy said. "But then I figured out musicians only get paid if they're good. The guy who tunes the piano gets paid every time."

"Mike, how was my Braille?" Everly asked.

"Et was feni," I replied.

Leroy laughed. "So, you ever met another blind man before?"

I laughed.

He didn't. He said, "I was fifteen before I knew there were other blind people fumbling around this world just like me."

"When I was little," I began, "Mom used to take me to see this elderly gentleman who lived across town. He was also born blind, and I learned a lot from him. But by the time I started school, Mom had three kids on her hands, and we didn't make it over there much anymore. Mr. Blake was his name. Nice man."

"What did you learn from being around him?" Everly asked.

"To put everything in the same place every time," Leroy answered for me.

"Yes, sir," I agreed emphatically.

"Hold up your head or you'll be stiff and sore when you do," Leroy added. "And your mama will spank you if you don't."

I smiled. "Mom didn't spank me, but she did tell me a billion times to hold up my head and face her when I talked to her."

Leroy went on. "Don't walk around with your tongue between your teeth."

I laughed knowingly.

Everly said, "I don't get it."

Leroy gave a slow chuckle. "Ever run your head into something when you're holding your tongue between your teeth? Ouch!" He continued. "Make friends with lots of people who drive cars."

I snickered. "Amen."

"Move slow because hitting your shin on a chair slow hurts less than hitting it fast," Leroy said.

"Nope. Not me. I could never go fast enough," I stated. "But I have rearranged my shins plenty of times."

He continued. "Get out of school as soon as possible because school is hard."

I slid off the bench. "Nope. Again, not me. I couldn't get enough of school. I love school. Still do. I get excited when the first day approaches."

"No, sir!" Leroy said as he took my place on the bench. "Not me!" He chuckled and began his work. As I was walking out of the room, he said, "Hey, Mike. I'm black."

I gasped. "No kidding? I thought you were orange!" Turning to Everly, I begged, "Do you have any idea of the significance of this?"

"What?" she asked.

Leroy laughed. "It means he's color blind, too!"

"You two are crazy," Everly said. "Mike, if you're done in here, could you give me a hand?"

"I could give you two," I replied, "but that's my limit. What do you need?"

As I followed her down the hall toward the front door, she spoke over her shoulder. "Grandma gave me some pumpkins from her garden. You like pumpkin pie?"

"Definitely."

"Good. You can help me carry them to the kitchen. Then we'll cut up a couple of them and bake them."

"Smashing," I said.

But when I realized that she intended for me to clean out the inside of the pumpkin, I wrinkled my lip and announced, "I'll pass."

She gave a little snort. "When I was a kid, we had a rule. If you don't help raise the produce, you don't get to help eat it."

"Then I will have to abdicate my portion of the pumpkin proceeds. I cleaned out a pumpkin once. Keep in mind that my fingertips are my eyes. Would you want pumpkin guts smeared in your eyes?"

Breaking her tough-guy, federal agent persona, Everly actually awarded me with a laugh. A genuine laugh. "Mike, I'm supposed to be protecting you. I'm supposed to be figuring out who's trying to kill you. And I'm supposed to remain professional about all this. But sometimes, man, you just crack me up!"

"Does that mean I still get a slice of pumpkin pie? Or two? Or six?" I implored.

Still wearing a smile, she relented, "You wash 'em. I'll gut 'em."

Chapter Eleven
⠀⠄⠂⠄ ⠏⠒⠭ ⠀⠄⠒⠁ ⠐⠇⠂⠒

Saturday night found me sitting at the piano playing around with a bluesy version of a melody I had heard Everly humming that morning.

She leaned into the room. "Your phone is ringing. Here you go."

I reached out for the device. "Hello?"

It was Derek. "Hey, we're at a wedding dance at the K of C Hall, and we thought you might like to come over."

There was a lot of background noise on his end. I asked, "You have a Kentucky Fried Chicken hall?"

"K *of* C. Not KFC. Knights of Columbus," he said, as though I should know that. "It's the Catholic men's organization. Surely you've heard of it."

"Sorry. I'm not Catholic."

"Jeez. Well, anyway, we thought you might like to come by and meet some locals and listen to the band. They've already put away the food, so the bride and her mother both said it was okay if we invited you. Otherwise, they'd never allow you in. You eat enough for six people."

"You're sure it's okay with the management?" I quipped.

"Yes. Actually, it was Tish's idea to ask. She thought you probably get lonely over there with no one but dogs for company."

I wasn't sure if Everly could hear his side of the conversation, so I ignored the comment. "What's the dress code?"

"It's ninety degrees in here, no kidding, so don't wear your suit. You'd sweat through it. Khaki slacks and a polo shirt would be fine. Running shoes are okay, too. I'm wearing mine."

Everly was still leaning in the doorway after I disconnected. She asked, "Are you going to the wedding dance downtown?"

"I guess so."

"That's too bad. I was enjoying the concert. That's one of my favorite songs."

"What is that song, by the way?" I entreated. "I'd never heard it until you sang it."

"It's an old English folk tune called 'Come All Ye Fair and Tender Maidens.' I'll sing it for you sometime. You better get ready to go."

Fifteen minutes later, I entered the hall with my hand resting on Tish's shoulder. During the drive, she had explained that Derek had been drinking, so he'd asked her to come fetch me.

She led me to the table where Derek was sipping beer from a plastic cup. He stood and slapped my shoulder. "Glad you could come. Hey, get a load of this."

He put my hand on Tish's belly.

My eyebrows flew upward. "Holy cow! She's about to blow!"

Tish giggled. "Have you ever felt a pregnant belly before?"

"My sister's. She let me feel my niece kicking inside her."

"Sorry. This kid is asleep right now," Tish said. "You'll have to feel for a kick later on."

For a half hour, Derek and I talked about running and running strategy and running courses and running shoes and runners. Then Tish touched my arm and said, "Mike, I'd like you to meet Kimberlyn Johnson, the second grade teacher at the local school. Kimberlyn, this is Mike Sands from the big city in California. Actually, his last name is Sandse—" She hesitated. "Mike, I don't know how to say your last name."

"Sandsebrotsky. But Sands works just fine." I replied as I stood and took Kimberlyn's hand. "It's nice to meet you." I asked how to spell her first name. And she asked if I knew how to dance.

"If you can get me to the dance floor, I can make a passable attempt," I claimed. "This sounds like a great jitterbug song."

"It is," she agreed as she took my hand and weaved us through the tables and chairs.

I prompted, "Just make sure we have a big acreage so I don't run you into anyone."

She assured me there were only two other couples on the floor, and they were both in far corners and doing less energetic steps.

One of the advantages of being a distance runner is that I can dance as long as I can run. Anyone who has spent an evening engaged in energetic swing-dancing knows it takes some endurance. It also causes women's clothes to shed. By the end of the fourth dance, Kimberlyn was clad only in a tank top and a flouncy, knee-length skirt.

After an hour on the floor, Kimberlyn and I found Derek and Tish yawning at their table. Minutes later, assured that Kimberlyn could give me a lift home, they left.

We danced as long as the band played. Then hand in
hand we walked three blocks to Kimberlyn's house to get
her car.

"I'm surprised to find a good dancer out here in the
sticks," she said as we walked.

"Oh?" I asked.

With a slight air of condescension, she relayed, "This
place is so backward. They think there are two kinds of
music. Country and rock."

"How long have you been here?" I probed.

"Two years. I don't know if I'll renew my contract at
the end of the year. I mean, I came here hoping to change
minds and hearts. But this place is still just as backward
now as when I got here."

Dripping with sarcasm, she added, "I mean, all the guys
here just want to show me their gun collection or take me
to church."

"Where are you from?" I asked.

"Liberty, Missouri," she answered.

"That's part of Kansas City?" I asked.

She shrugged and said for purposes of conversation,
yes.

When we were settled in her front seat, I asked, "Is
there a good steakhouse around here? Someplace we could
go for dinner sometime? I mean supper."

She put the car in reverse and eased it onto the street.
"Um. I thought you and Everly Galloway were dating,
Mike."

"Just roommates," I asserted.

"Oh. Well, in that case, yes. There is a decent place here
in town, kind of a burger joint. But there's a steakhouse
about twenty miles from here. And there's a nice Mexican
restaurant in that same town."

"I'll make you a deal. I'll buy. You drive."

She giggled. "Not the other way around?"

I shrugged. "It might take longer that way. Hard to drive with one hand on the wheel and the other swinging the white cane out the window."

"How long have you been teaching?" she asked.

"I was in the classroom for three years. Administration since then," I answered.

"I'm surprised you can do that," she mused. "But I'm sure glad to meet someone here who isn't a hick."

"Hick?" I asked with a grin.

"Yeah! I mean, around here they think diversity means having collard greens *and* turnip greens in the same meal. They're all a bunch of homophobic bigots."

I didn't know how to respond to that. So I didn't.

She asked if I would come talk to her second graders soon.

"Sure, I'd love to. Would an afternoon work?"

We set up a time. She told me how to get to her classroom. Then she pulled up at Everly's place. But she didn't turn off the engine. I thanked her for the ride. She said no problem.

Then without so much as a handshake, I stood there as she drove away.

Inside the house, Everly put down her magazine and asked, "How was the dance? And who brought you home?"

Instead of answering—which I didn't feel obligated to do—I asked, "What exactly is a hick?"

She snorted. "Only a city slicker would ask."

"No, really," I pressed. "I just got a lecture about hicks. So I'm wondering exactly what constitutes a hick."

Everly pulled out her phone and recited a definition. "A hick is someone who lives in the country, is unintelligent, and provincial."

I pondered that for a moment and wondered if Kimberlyn knew the definition of *provincial*. I asked Everly if she did.

Without referencing the phone, she replied, "Provincial refers to one who lives in the outlying regions. The British often referred to those residing in their colonies as positively provincial." The last two words were delivered with a pompous British accent.

I nodded and observed, "You don't seem unintelligent or provincial."

"Why, thank you. That's the nicest thing anyone's said to me all day."

"Has anyone said anything to you all day?" I probed.

"Moo. Woof-woof. I think there were a couple of meows in there."

Before I drifted off that night, I wondered if I would see Kimberlyn again. Or if I wanted to.

In the end, I decided I did want to. Because unlike with Everly, I had at least a chance of getting a kiss from her.

On our morning run, Derek pelted me with questions about the remainder of the dance, my ride home, and whether I made it to any bases.

Struck out, I confessed. But today is another day.

Back to the house in time to get ready for church, I showered and shaved and put on the same clothes I would have put on five days of the week had I been in California. But here, I wore a suit only to church.

As we walked out to her pickup, Everly asked a question that floored me. "Will you go to church when you get back home?"

"You mean, like, every week?" I returned. "Well, I um. No. I don't think so. I mean, it's your church. I'm just visiting."

"Not really," she said. "No one has sole ownership of God. He belongs to all of us. Or, rather, we all belong to Him. And since when do you employ the overuse of the word *like*? Did you pick that up from your little urchins at school?"

In my best valley girl impersonation, I crooned, "Oh, I'm all like, no way, and she was, like, *whatever*, and I was all like, get out!"

She rewarded me with a rare chuckle. "You do that pretty well. You sure you aren't gay?"

"You shouldn't slap a blind person. It's not polite," I warned.

We entered the back of the church and were greeted by the pastor. "Good morning, Everly. Hi, Dr. Mike."

"Good morning, Reverend Mike," I replied. We had had fun with the fact that we shared a name. As a kid, I had once asked my parents why they saddled me with the single most commonly used American male name of the Twentieth Century. Dad had answered that I was pretty ordinary, so they thought it appropriate.

"Say, Mike," the reverend asked, "I meant to call you earlier this week, but I got sidetracked and forgot. Now that you're a member of the congregation, I wondered if we could press you into service this weekend to read the scriptures."

Tilting my head slightly toward Everly, I wondered if she had quietly texted the minister to put him up to this, considering our very recent conversation. But I had been with her the whole time, and I didn't think she had been texting and driving.

"Well," I began slowly, "only if you have the readings in Braille, I'm afraid."

"I do. I ordered a Braille Bible a few weeks ago, and it finally came in. Today's readings are nothing out of the ordinary. No fourteen-generation genealogies, no mention of the Melchizedek heritage, no geographical locations. So you won't stumble over any pronunciations. I have the correct readings marked with sticky notes, so you'll know where to start and stop. You just begin by saying, 'A reading from the Book of Whatever' and then read the verses. Okay? Oh, and the Bible is yours to keep. It's not like it would do anyone else any good around here."

I was stalling for time to think of a way out of this. As I had just told Everly this morning, this wasn't my schtick. "That must be a pretty hefty tome," I commented.

Reverend Mike agreed, "It will build your muscles. It's in a binder, though, so I suppose you could separate it into Old and New Testaments."

Realizing that I was now the proud owner of a Bible—for the first time in my life—I said, "Please let me reimburse you."

"Sure. It was free."

"Really?" I asked. Then that was that. Relenting to the task, I said, "I will need someone to lead me to the altar. Or the pulpit. Or whatever it's called."

"I'm sure Everly would do that. Everly?"

"No problem," she said. "I haven't run him into anything lately. I can probably handle it."

"Great," Reverend Mike emoted. "While he's reading, you just stand to the side. After his first reading, you step up to the mic and read the responses. Then Mike, you will do the second reading. Then you can both sit down. Thanks, you two. Come with me. I'll show you your Bible."

I think they shared a wink.

After the opening song and during some kind of prayer, I skimmed through the readings. Then I stepped out of the pew and put my hand farther above Everly's elbow than I ordinarily would. Usually, I used her shoulder. But this way I could bump her ribcage and whatever else was nearby. I didn't think she would slap me in front of the whole church.

After she deposited me at the lectern, Everly reached in front of me to adjust the microphone. Then I began. It wasn't like public speaking was anything new to me. But the cadence of the scriptures was slightly different than I was used to. I managed not to bungle too much.

At the end of the first reading, I stepped sideways and let Everly have the mic. Then I did the second reading.

Something about reading the Bible passages aloud in front of all these people made it real to me. Suddenly, this wasn't just Everly's church. It wasn't Pastor Mike's church. It wasn't Shelley and Gunnar's church.

Suddenly, in some small way, it was *my* church. It was my scripture. It was my God. It was my Bible.

In fact, this particular Bible had not only been written for a blind person, but had been given to *me*.

To me.

And for a little while, I didn't feel quite so blind.

Until later in the day when I talked to Dad on the phone.

He told me the police had established the identity of the dead man in my house. Carlos Burleson. He asked if that rang any bells.

"No," I told him. "Should it?"

Dad explained, "He got out of prison four days before he was shot in your house."

"Why was he in jail?" I asked.

"Aggravated rape."

I pondered that. "So it isn't a stretch to assume he would kidnap and murder a girl."

"He raped her, too," Dad reported.

I wanted to vomit.

"Mike, you know the real name of your friend Charles is Zana Kazemi, right? As in Top Ten Wanted Terrorist list?"

"So I've heard. But it's a different guy. Everly told me the real terrorist is between twenty-eight and thirty-two years old and has been in Pakistan for the past two years."

"Yes," he agreed. "That's the same thing I found out. Same name, but definitely not the same guy."

Fiddling around on the piano and stewing over the conversation with Dad, I heard Everly answer the front door. Then I heard my name.

When I appeared in the living room, the vet asked, "Howdy, Mike. You want to feel some tits?"

My face froze.

He laughed. "I thought you might like to take a guided tour of a cow. A real tame cow. My sister hand milks a little Jersey. The thing thinks it's a house pet. She asked me to invite you over to meet Gertie."

Confused, I asked, "The cow invited me to meet your sister? Or your sister invited me to meet the cow?"

He bellowed, "My sister Linda invited you to meet the cow Gertie. Damned school teachers! Always getting after a guy about his grammar. You want to come with me?"

"Love to." To Everly, I asked, "Do I have a kitchen pass?"

"Sure. Doc carries a gun. You'll be safe enough."

"You do?" I asked him with surprise.

As he led me toward the door, he said, "I carry a .38 in the pickup in case I have to euthanize a bovine or a would-be drug thief. See, I carry some highly sought after drugs that some thugs would like to snort or shoot up or whatever it is they do with them. Can you get down the stairs okay?"

"Unless Everly moved them recently," I replied.

We climbed into his truck and headed down the driveway. Twenty minutes and a lot of banter later, we pulled into his sister's place.

She met me with a hearty handshake (calloused hands like Everly's) and led the way to the barn. Gertie was tiny compared to the beef cows I had met at Everly's grandparents' place. She was also inquisitive and hungry. Once some grain was dumped into her feed bunk, she paid no more attention to me.

Linda invited me to feel Gertie all over, which I did, including the ear tag that felt like a giant plastic earring, the prominent hip bones jutting through the leather hide, and the sandbur on her rump.

Then I got down to the udder. "So this is the business part?"

Linda laughed. "That's right."

"How much milk comes out of a cow in a day?" I asked.

"At this stage of production—which is four months past freshening—she's giving about three gallons at each milking. That's six gallons a day."

"Wow!" I exclaimed. "From this little tiny thing? She's hardly bigger than Napili, the dog!"

"A Holstein would produce a lot more. And she'd outweigh Gertie by double," Linda pointed out. She took my hand and held it as high as my shoulder. "And she'd stand about this high at the withers."

Then Doc grunted, "Teach the poor kid to milk. I promised him he'd get his hands on some tits today."

Apparently Linda found nothing out of the ordinary in the request. She plunked me down on the milking stool and taught me to milk the cow.

I lasted about a minute and a half before my muscles were screaming at me to stop. "This is tough on the forearms," I pointed out.

"It takes getting used to," Linda agreed. "Once you practice a little, you'll build up those muscles and be able to milk for the rest of your life, even if you only do it once in a while. You want to meet the chickens when we're done here?"

I was introduced to the chickens, most of whom fluttered and flapped away when we entered the hen house. But two or three came right up to us. Those were the pets,

Linda explained. She said if they weren't so tame and friendly, they would have been in the CrockPot by now.

I shuddered.

We knelt and I ran my hands over the silky feathers. Then I reached into the laying boxes and collected eggs so fresh that some were still warm.

From the doorway, Doc mentioned, "This won't impress you, Mike, but some of those eggs are a dull green color. Some are brown. Some are white."

Scowling, I asked, "Does the egg color depend on what you feed them?"

"It depends on the breed," Linda explained. "The shells are made the same way, no matter the color. Diet does matter for shell integrity, though. Most of these eggshells are much thicker and harder than a store-bought egg."

Finished with the chicken demonstration, we went inside for coffee cake (after hand-washing) and coffee. Then Doc got a call to meet someone in the clinic.

HBC dog, he said. Linda seemed to know what that meant. I didn't learn it until we were on the way to his office. Hit By Car.

I tried to stay out of the way once we arrived. But Doc led me into the darkroom and showed me how to develop an x-ray.

"You think you can do one by yourself?" he asked, "because I need to take a few more films, and I don't have a tech to help me."

"I think so," I answered.

"Good. Come over here." He put my hand on a light switch and said, "Don't flip this switch. Got it? Right now we're both in the dark. But if you hit this light, you'll ruin the films."

"Got it."

He left the room. A few minutes later, I heard him deposit an exposed film into the metal box that was built into the wall separating the x-ray room from the darkroom. He had explained that the box could be accessed from only one side at a time so that light couldn't enter the darkroom.

When he closed the box on the other side, I opened it and went through the checklist.

Ten minutes later, I had developed five x-rays.

Four college degrees, teacher, principal, superintendent, competitive runner, and now I could add x-ray developer to my resume.

The next morning after I filled in Derek on my Sunday afternoon, I told him about my impending talk with the second graders. He reminded me that his oldest child was a second grader. And sure enough, when I walked into the second grade room that afternoon, I heard a startled voice squeak, "Uncle Mike!"

Kimberlyn introduced me and found me a tiny chair, and I began with my typical second-grade spiel. As always, the most fun part of the presentation was the question and answer session.

The ubiquitous, "How do you drive?" was the second question. They also wanted a demonstration of my cell phone and were suitably impressed with how it worked without the screen lighted. Did I have a guide dog? How did I find my way around? How did I get dressed?

How did I brush my teeth? With my most sincere voice, I asked the petitioner, "Can you see your teeth when you brush them?"

"In a mirror," he replied.

Very seriously, I said, "I never look in the mirror when I brush my teeth." That elicited some tittering.

Do I know what colors are? Am I sad that I'm blind? How long have I been blind? How did I learn to tie my shoes? Do I have bionic hearing?

Then there was a new one: how did I know when it was time to wash the windows?

What color are my eyes? What would I like to see if I could see? Do I have brothers and sisters, and are they blind, too? Do I dream? Are my dreams in color?

Then came a question that I usually got from older people: how did my parents find out I was blind?

I gave a very truncated recitation of the story I had heard only recently from Mom.

Accompanied by giggles, there were the typical bathroom questions. Then someone asked how did I read? How did I wash dishes? How did I make my cane shorter and longer? The answer to that one required a demonstration. They seemed impressed.

How did I watch TV? How did I check email? How did I take out the trash? How did I clean up after my dog. That elicited more giggling—especially after I explained that if I didn't clean it up right away, I might step in it.

How did I eat? How did I go to school? How did I go shopping?

The next question was how do I run? I addressed the question to Bette who very competently described how her daddy held one end of a cord while I held the other.

When my time was up (and then some), all the students in the town's entire second grade—all twenty-one of them—walked me to the door and bid me goodbye. I think they waved, too.

The next morning, I greeted Derek and asked about his ovaries.

He laughed. "I still can't believe Gunnar said that! Yeah, we're going back today again. Tish is ready to be done. But it's too early. She gets antsy to have it over with. Oh, and happy birthday."

"Thanks," I grinned as we trotted toward Gunnar's place.

We ran fifteen miles with a brief stop for coffee, toast, and eggs. When we came back to Shelley's dining room after the track workout, she had a full-fledged feast on the table. Tish was there with the kids. And with a birthday cake. Chocolate cake with chocolate whipped cream icing. Outstanding!

There were even a couple presents to open. When I opened the gift from Gunnar, he leaned forward on his chair and demanded, "You like it? Will it work?"

My fingers felt the sleek fabric of a racing singlet. "It's nice," I said. "What color is it?"

"Red, white, and blue. Like a flag," Tish supplied. "The front is blue with silver-white lettering, and the back is red and white striped."

"Thanks," I relayed with a smile. Then I asked, "What do the letters say?"

"Can't you feel them?" Gunnar asked. "They're reflective. But I had them weave the reflective stuff in so it doesn't feel tacky against your skin when you race. Can you read it?"

I ran my fingers across the surface and shook my head slowly. "No, I can't feel the letters. Like you said, they are woven into the fabric."

"It's just like my singlet," Derek announced, "except mine has white stars on the blue background. Yours says BLIND in all caps."

With a grin, I said, "So I won't have to wear the vest when I race."

"Exactly." Gunnar sounded pleased. "The vest causes too much drag. I mean, I know it isn't a lot physics-wise, but it's something. And every little bit counts."

Turning toward my racing partner, I said, "So we match."

"Like two aces in a deck of cards," he replied with pride.

With Derek off again to take his wife to the obstetrician, I was left at Everly's place on my own. I did my floor workout. Then I finished another Louis L'Amour book. Then, knowing I should go over the deposition transcripts I'd received that morning in the Stoltz case, but more than willing to procrastinate on my birthday, I walked out onto the porch. Napili came up and bumped my hand with his nose.

"Do you think I should pet you?" I asked. He didn't answer. But when I inquired, "Want to go for a run?" he began prancing. When I leaned down to pet him, he lurched upward and bopped my nose with his head. It wasn't the first time. His momma was just as bad.

"Oaf," I grunted. "Okay. Hang on."

I went back inside and found a pad of sticky notes near the kitchen phone. Hoping the second sheet was blank, I flipped to it and fished around in the silverware drawer for a pen, clicked it on, and hoped I wrote, "Going running with Napili." Writing a note when you can't see what you're writing can result in interesting outcomes.

The note reminded me of my college days when a group of my friends got together at least one night a week to play Pictionary, a board game in which a player selects a card bearing a word which he then has a set period of time to wordlessly draw in an attempt to enable his partners to guess the word. A rule was instituted that when I was among the group playing, everyone had to draw with eyes closed. Me included.

It was one of the rules.

Fortunately, one of my industrious—and obviously bored—friends took it upon himself to label each card with Braille so I didn't have to rely on someone to whisper my word to me.

Adhering the sticky note to the table, I grabbed a leash and went back outside.

In the cool, dry sunshine and very slight breeze, the sounds of our feet made a nice rhythm on the running trail Everly had built.

But three miles from Everly's house, something else added to the percussion section.

Napili began barking and lunging toward the rattling reptile.

I froze in my tracks and held fast to the leash. With my free hand, I fumbled for my phone.

Derek's voice came on the line saying, "Hey, Mike, I can't talk. We're just—*oh, man!* Is that a rattler?"

"I'm sending you video," I said shakily. "You tell me which way to go."

A few seconds later, he said, "Okay, you need to—wait a second. Turn around and show me video behind you. If this is their breeding season, there might be another one around."

Without moving my feet, I pivoted my body and showed him the view behind me.

His voice relaxing slightly, he said, "Okay. The snake in front of you is coiled right in the middle of the road. It's chilly today; it was probably sunning itself. So go back the way you came. Okay?"

I tugged on Napili's leash. He stood fast. So I yanked. Into the phone, I said, "Thanks, bro."

Only five minutes after the snake encounter, Napili again went nuts. There was no buzzing from a rattler this time. The big dog bounded off the trail, taking me with him for a few strides.

Then my shins ran into a wicked plant composed of jagged daggers. Everly had told me yucca grew in this pasture. I was certain I had just encountered some.

Tripping and losing grasp of the leash, I somersaulted and skidded on the hard, dry grass.

Too near to me, the fight between Napili and his adversary rose to heightened pitch. Snapping jaws. Gnashing teeth. Guttural growls.

For my part, I jumped to my feet and waved my arms and yelled, just in case whatever it was decided the dog was too much for it and came after me.

Then Napili shrieked. Shrieked again. Then he sprinted away, yipping with every bound.

My phone was in my hands now. Derek didn't answer. I tried Everly. Before she even spoke, I snapped, "*What is that?*"

I swung the phone to one side then the other.

"Slow down," she chastised. "All I'm getting is blur."

I snapped, "Napili just had a fight with something. What is it?"

She was silent for a few agonizingly long seconds as I stood there wondering if I were about to be attacked by some vicious wild animal.

"I don't see anything," she said calmly.

Too calmly.

I took a deep breath. Then another. Then I said, "It attacked him. Or he attacked it. Anyway, Napili ran away, and I'm stranded."

"Okay. Can you make it to the house if I get you back on the road?"

"I think so," I said without any certainty.

"Hold your phone straight in front of you."

I did.

"Now shift the camera to your right. Slowly."

I complied.

"Okay. The road is on your right. I have to hang up now, but call back if you need to."

I let out another shaky breath and thanked her.

Then I began slowly working my way back to the road. I should have asked her how far it was. But I hadn't. And pride kept me from ringing her back.

Taking baby steps, I carefully eased my weight onto each foot. On about the twentieth step, I shifted my weight onto my left foot.

And the ground gave way.

Two or three ragged cartwheels later, I came to a rest on a stretch of coarse sand. My sweatshirt was up around my face, and my back was scraped. Pushing myself to a sitting position, I carefully assessed my body parts. All accounted for. But my knees and elbows were skinned and already beginning to ooze.

Swallowing a curse, I reached again for my phone.

It was gone!

Panic is what kills people in the water.

At least I wasn't in the water. I could breathe. So I didn't need to panic.

But I sure wanted to.

I called to the phone. If it were near enough, it would pick up my voice.

It wasn't.

I got to my feet and—with thoughts of rattlesnakes still very fresh in my mind—pondered the best course of action. It seemed that I had fallen into some sort of dry waterway. One possible action was to walk downstream until I came to—came to what? I had no idea where this creek led. And it might have tangles of deadfalls and jumbles of rocks.

And rattlesnakes.

A shudder ran through me.

Then the phone rang!

It was somewhere to my right and above me. Scrambling as quickly as I could and taking care not to fall again, I moved toward it.

It stopped ringing.

"Call me back!" I beseeched.

A few seconds later, the device complied and began ringing again.

By the time it stopped ringing this time, I was almost near enough to activate it by voice.

It began ringing again almost immediately. "Hello?" I yelled.

"Mike, where are you?" Everly asked faintly.

"I fell in a dry creek bed," I called.

There was silence. After half a minute, she asked, "Why the hell did you do that?"

At that instant, I felt as near crying as I had in years.

By the time she spoke again, I had located the phone. She asked, "What are you wearing?"

Exasperated, I snapped, "What is this? An obscene phone call? I'm wearing a toga. A bathrobe. A Speedo. Why does it matter what I'm wearing?"

"Do you know what color you're wearing?" she asked patiently. For some reason, when one person in a conversation is losing his mind and the other person is calm, it makes the berserk person more berserk. She added, "It'll help me spot you."

I sat on the slope of the crumbling bank. "I don't have any idea." I omitted the expletive that popped into my frazzled mind.

An hour later, I tripped on the way up the porch steps and was reminded of the skinned knees.

"You sure you're okay?" Everly asked for the seventh time.

"Peachy," I grumbled on my way to the shower.

When I emerged from my room in jeans, boots, a polo shirt, and a sports jacket, Everly asked, "Are you going somewhere?"

"Yes."

278

She waited for elaboration. Finally, she asked, "Are you going out with Kimberlyn?"

"Yes."

"Oh. Okay. I guess I'll put this in the fridge, then."

I downed a glass of water and said, "I'm sorry. I should've alerted the chef that I have a date."

"It's no problem." She had been nice to me since extracting me from the drink. But she hadn't afforded my sudden and unbidden accommodations with the word *creek* or even *wash*. She had called it a ditch. Drainage ditch, to be precise.

It had seemed much more alarming than a simple ditch.

Still in a dour mood, I tried to put on a chipper attitude when Kimberlyn picked me up. I asked about her class, her curriculum, her parents, siblings, fellow teachers, administrators, and anything else I thought would keep her talking.

She seemed happy to talk about herself. Most people are.

When we stepped into the restaurant, Kimberlyn immediately said, "Oh! It's, like, freezing in here."

"Here," I offered as I started to slip off my jacket. "You can wear this."

"Oh, no. I'll be fine. It's just that some places keep the air conditioning so cold. And it's already cold outside. Aren't you chilly?"

I said I was fine.

She looked around for a moment and said, "Follow me."

I reached for her shoulder, but she was gone.

Finally a waiter offered me an elbow and led me to the table where Kimberlyn was already reading a menu. On the way, he verified that they had no Braille menus.

After the server had taken our drink order, I asked Kimberlyn more questions about her life.

Several minutes after the steaks arrived, a manager dropped by to ask if everything was to our satisfaction. Fortunately it was a male manager. I asked if he could lead me to the men's room.

I rested my left hand on his right shoulder which worked fine until he ran me into a chair, a chair occupied by a man. I apologized. The manager apologized. The man in the chair grunted.

When I ask a stranger to lead me to the restroom, they fear I will need help once I'm there. To ease the manager's concerns en route, I suggested, "Tell me the layout before we get there, so you can just leave me at the door."

Relief plain in his voice, he complied and then happily disappeared.

Back out in the dining room, I snapped open my cane and held it relatively upright so that it only probed the area immediately in front of me. If I had been outdoors or in an open area where I could move faster, I would have held it out flatter in order to cover more territory. I made it halfway back to Kimberlyn before a customer backed into me.

The chain reaction that resulted must have been humorous to watch.

It was not humorous to me. Maybe it would be in a year. But it was desperately embarrassing at the time.

I tripped and fell immediately in the path of a waiter carrying a huge tray of plates.

It just wasn't my day.

Rattlesnakes. Drainage ditches. And now a massive melee in a nice steakhouse with a girl who would probably never speak to me again.

Back on my feet, I apologized profusely. Someone handed me my cane. Someone else pointed me toward Kimberlyn who was probably hiding under the table.

A few minutes later when our waitress came by to check on us, I quietly slipped her my credit card. "I want to pay the tab for the table whose dinner I scattered all over the floor."

"Oh, are you sure? There are nine in that party," she squeaked. "And they are drinking. A lot. It's gonna be a pretty hefty check."

"I'm sure," I replied.

She took my card and returned a few minutes later with a slip for me to sign. Evidently she had worked with blind customers before because she held the slip and placed my hand on the signature line. I thanked her. She left.

Kimberlyn tried to keep the conversation going. But it was uphill.

Then a couple of big guys approached our table. One of them clapped a hand on my shoulder and, with a jovial, booming voice, announced, "Hey, buddy! That was the funniest thing I've seen in this place since—well, since forever, I reckon. And you sure don't have to pick up our tab. Let me pay for it."

Coming to my feet, which made me recall my sore knees, I held out a hand. "No, sir. It's on me. I hope I didn't wreck your evening."

He shook my hand and laughed. The other one bellowed, "Ah, hell! We was already into the most important part. We was pretty well lit by the time we got around to ordering food. Hell, Pard, you come join us anytime." He slipped a business card into my hand. "Give us a call. You folks have a nice night, now."

When Kimberlyn pulled up in front of Everly's house, I reached for the door handle.

She put a hand on my arm. "Mike, thank you for the nice meal."

Dubiously, I asked, "Really?"

She smiled. "Yes. You're a really good conversationalist. I realized on the way home that you asked me all about myself tonight, but you never said anything about yourself. So how was your day after you left my classroom?"

I leaned back against the head rest. "Thanks for asking. I almost stepped on a rattlesnake and then fell into a ditch. Just a normal, routine day."

Caressing my arm, she asserted, "Tomorrow will be better."

"It will," I said with a weak smile. "Thanks."

"I'm just so sorry that you, that you can't see." I had a feeling she was about to add, "If it weren't for that, you'd be quite a catch." But she didn't.

Trying to ignore the sympathy—which I neither needed nor wanted—I murmured, "I'm sure tomorrow will be a great day if I have a goodnight kiss to reminisce about."

Her hand stopped moving on my arm. "Mike, I—I'm not sure I—I mean, I have a reputation to uphold. I mean, I have certain criterions that I have to think of. I mean, you're a nice guy. You're really smart and everything. But you just. . . well, you move your hands weird, and your face and stuff. And you do stuff that just. . ." She mercifully stopped.

Or at least I cut her off when I pushed open the door and stepped outside. Napili's wet muzzle found my hand instantly. "Have a nice evening." I closed the door and walked up the sidewalk. Inside the house, I kicked a laundry basket.

Everly jumped up from the couch to move it. "Sorry, Mike."

"Cowboy boots do have advantages," I muttered as I went to my room. Teeth brushed, boots off, clothes changed, I fell on the bed and lay there for over an hour.

Finally, I got up to go to the bathroom. On my return, I overheard Everly talking quietly on the phone.

For some reason, I stood just inside my door to eavesdrop. Her words were low, but I was pretty sure she was making a report on the investigation.

An hour after I finally fell asleep, Everly was beside me. "Mike? Are you okay?"

Shaking and sweating, I was sitting bolt upright on the bed.

"Did you have a nightmare?" she plied.

I swallowed hard and began vigorously rubbing both eyes.

"Mike? You okay?" she asked again.

"I'm okay."

"Were you dreaming? Stop digging at your eyes." She put her hands on my shoulders. "Stop it."

Dropping my hands to my lap, I muttered, "I'm sorry I woke you."

"I wasn't asleep yet. What were you dreaming about?"

"Don't you ever sleep?"

"Not yet," she answered. "I don't run thirty miles a day. Don't need as much rest as you do."

I fell back on the pillow and muttered, "I hate electric cars."

She didn't move. After a moment, she asked, "What are you talking about?"

"Electric cars. They don't make noise. They just clobber you." Not only had I dreamed of being hit by an electric car, but Dolores Stoltz had been driving it.

Kimberlyn had been in the passenger seat.

After hovering uncertainly for another minute, Everly rose and left. "Good night."

When Derek arrived the next morning, I reached into the pocket of my shorts and found no tether. "Hang on," I said. Leaving him on the front porch, I returned to my room and fished through all my pockets.

Still no tether.

Back on the porch, I explained why I had left him waiting.

"Oh. Is that the problem?" he asked sardonically. "Actually, your tether is all over the yard in little pieces. I thought maybe you had a spare."

I dropped my chin to my chest, a maneuver my sister had taught me during all those hours miming television actors. Deleting a mental expletive, I stepped back inside and called, "Everly? Do you have anything we can use for a tether? Something stretchy and about a yard long?"

Passing me on the way to her pickup, she hopped up on the rail of the bed and reached into the melee of junk she carried everywhere. "How about a bungee cord?"

When I took it, I grimaced. "Do you have one that isn't soaked in grease?"

"Probably not," she replied coolly.

I thanked her without much enthusiasm.

When we trotted onto the road, Derek told me every detail of the obstetric visit the previous day. He relayed Bette's report about my visit to her classroom. He told me everything his kids had done the previous evening. He told me every detail of the supper his wife had prepared the previous night.

Five miles into the run, he suddenly turned toward me. "Okay. What's up? I left you at least three openings to ding me with a one-liner. And you passed up every opportunity. The tether is no big deal. I kinda like the bungee better anyway. It has more body."

"And more grease," I added.

"Yeah. More grease. And I like the metal hook on your end. I wish it was a little shorter so we could both have a hook. It's easier to hold. So what's up?"

I didn't answer for a while. I didn't want to answer at all.

Finally, he prodded, "Come on. What's eating you? Why are you suddenly so quiet? It's very unlike you. I thought you said teachers will die if they don't talk at least every ten minutes."

"I almost stepped on a rattlesnake yesterday," I said by way of explanation.

"Yeah. But you're still walking around today, so you didn't get bit. What else?"

"I fell in a creek."

"Holy cow! What creek?" he demanded.

I gestured vaguely toward the east. "Over there."

He glanced "over there". "You fell in the drainage ditch?"

I didn't answer. Didn't need to.

"How did you manage that?"

"Napili abandoned me," I grumbled. "He pulled me off my feet, jerked the leash from my hand, and had a fight with a porcupine. He ran off to the house. Everly told me later that his face and paws were full of quills."

"Better him than you," Derek noted. "So how did you get back?"

"Everly had to quit shoeing her horse or whatever she was doing and come find me. She couldn't see me until she was a few feet from the ditch because it's so deep."

He pondered that for several strides. Then he suddenly asked, "Didn't you have a date last night with Kimberlyn? How did that go?"

"I tripped a waiter."

He waited. When it was clear I had no more to say, he asked, "And?"

"And he was carrying a big platter full of dishes. What do you think?"

He laughed. "How did Kimberlyn handle it?"

"I'll be surprised if she doesn't slip out of town quietly in the night, never to be seen in Nebraska again."

He laughed again. A few minutes later, he asked, "Mike, do you have feelings for Everly?"

"Did you know she's employed to protect me?"

"I don't know any details." A few strides later, he said, "I knew she used to work for the FBI and that she moved into her uncle's house shortly before you got here. But that doesn't answer my question."

"That's her uncle's house? Where is her uncle?" I asked.

"Her aunt and uncle's youngest kid graduated from high school in May. They left for Haiti or the Dominican Republic or someplace on a church mission shortly before Everly got here. I got wind that they had wanted to make the trip but wouldn't leave without someone to take care of the ranch. When she said she could come, they bought their tickets."

"So her uncle runs the place? Not her grandpa?" I inquired.

"I don't really know. So are you attracted to her, or what?"

"What does that have to do with Kimberlyn?"

He slugged my shoulder. "Quit being a butthead. Do you have a thing for Everly or not?"

"What's your point?"

"I'm just trying to figure out why this deal last night bothered you so much. I think your biological clock is ticking. You've started thinking you need to pair up and start a family."

I laughed sardonically. "I'm not Catholic, remember? I don't feel a need to single-handedly repopulate the State of Nebraska."

"Come on," he said. "All species are programmed to procreate. It's the natural order of things."

286

I had no more to say. But a few minutes before we got to Gunnar's place, Derek stated, "You're coming to our house for dinner tonight. Forget the second grade teacher. She's a little on the weird side anyway. I told Tish I wasn't sure she should introduce you in the first place."

"Why?" I asked.

"She has a nose ring," he said as though it was obvious.

I waited. He said no more. I asked, "What about it?"

"Listen, when God created the world, he gave America a shake and everything loose fell into California. It's where all the fruits and nuts came to rest. But out here, people with tattoos and dreadlocks and so many pieces of metal stuck in their faces that they look like they had a bad wreck with an open tackle box in their laps are just plain weird. We admit it. We don't have to sit around and pretend we think they're okay and squawk about diversity. Besides, diversity is just a word that says we have to accept the weirdos and make fun of the normal people."

Fully aware that he was trying to goad me into a political debate, I said, "Which category are you in? Weirdo or normal?"

He laughed and said, "That's more like it. Come over tonight. We'll put some normal in your life."

A minute later, I felt the ground sloping to my right. "Hey," I entreated, "are we planning to go off-road?"

"Oh, sorry." He eased us back onto the level center of the track.

"What are you gawking at?" I implored.

His face was pointed to our left. He didn't answer for a while. "I saw something on the ridge. Just over the horizon. I can't quite make it out."

I scowled. "Like what? Like someone with a rifle and a scope?"

"No," he answered absently. After another minute, he sighed. "It's Everly. She's on a horse. She must be riding parallel to us just over the crest of the hill."

I thought about that for a while. "You mean she's watching us, or what?"

He shrugged. "I don't know. But I guess she wouldn't take a shot at us, so we're okay. Right?"

When I walked into Derek's home that evening, Tish was scurrying around the kitchen and began apologizing right away that supper wasn't ready.

"Don't sweat it. I don't think I'll starve to death in the next thirty seconds," I assured her as my hand was grasped by a tiny one.

Tugging me toward the living room, seven-year-old Bette said, "Come on, Uncle Mike. We have the farm all set up. Are you coming to see us at school again? Everybody loved you!"

I heard the tab on an aluminum can a moment before Derek pressed the drink into my hand. "You like Bud?" he asked.

"Sure," I replied to both of them, though I didn't have plans to return to Kimberlyn's classroom and didn't particularly like Budweiser. "Where do I put this while I'm playing farm?"

After I took a drink, I held out the can for him to take. Then I wondered if the motion would have caused Kimberlyn embarrassment. I would have to inform my sister that despite all her hours of training, I still looked and moved like a blind guy.

The oversized coffee table/play table in their living room was covered with a series of tiny corrals and horses and cattle and cowboys and a big barn and trucks and tractors.

After I sank onto the carpet next to the table, Bette gently brushed my fingertips along the top of the corral.

"This is where we keep the horses. And this little pen over here is for the milk cow."

"Did I mention that Tish is from around here?" Derek grinned from his recliner. "Her folks make sure our kids are inculcated in agriculture at every opportunity. Bette even has her own horse, don't you, Sweetie?"

Brightly, she exuded, "His name is Bon-Bon, and he's bay, and he's really nice, and he lets me braid his mane while I'm sitting on his back, and I can slide off his butt and use his tail to go skiing! You have to come meet him sometime."

"Would he like Honu?" I plied. "And what is a bay? Is that a type of horse?"

"It's a color," she explained patiently. "It means he has a reddish-brown body and black points. Points are mane and tail. So his long hairs are black. And so are the bottoms of his legs."

"What color are his hooves?" I asked.

She slapped me on the arm. "They're black, silly! They only have white hooves if they have white on their lower legs. Like a sock or a stocking. Do you know the difference between a sock and a stocking?"

"What do you think of the farm set, Uncle Mike?" Derek asked to save me from admitting I didn't know the difference between a sock and a stocking.

"Nice barn," I said as I ran my hands over it. "What are these X's for on the doors?"

Bette explained patiently, "They are painted white. The rest of the barn is red. Back in the olden days, Grandpa said red paint was cheaper, so all the barns got painted red because it takes a lot of paint to paint a whole barn. But people painted the braces white. Does that make sense?"

"Does it make it easier to find your barn if it has white X's painted on the doors? Because otherwise, I can see where it might be easy to lose a barn."

Bette giggled and turned toward her dad. "Daddy, he's funny!"

At least I still had charms with some of the female population.

"What is this?" I asked as I picked up a plastic figure.

"It's a bucking bull," she offered.

"Wow," I said as my fingers examined the animal's splayed legs and twisted spine. "I'm glad I'm not trying to ride this thing."

"His rider already got bucked off. He's on the ground by that other fence."

I nodded with appreciation. "Poor guy."

She giggled again.

Derek was right. My soul needed some kid interaction.

And maybe he was right that I might someday like to have a house full of kids of my own.

That thought led me to melancholy as I contemplated the supreme challenge of having them by myself.

Again, I picked up one of the toys and asked, "Bette, what is this?"

"It's the working chute. That's where we process the cattle when we brand the calves and give the cows shots and stuff."

Examining the tiny version of a cattle chute was indeed instructive for me.

"Does it make more sense in a three-inch model than in the real size?" Derek asked from his chair.

"Infinitely," I answered. "When I was a kid, Dad bought me all kinds of models. I have a tiny Eiffel Tower, an Empire State Building, US Capitol, all kinds of animals, El Capitan, trains, trucks, cars, you name it. But," I nodded to Bette, "I never had a bucking bull or a barn or corrals like this. This is very helpful to me. It would take me a very long time to feel a real barn all over."

Again, she rewarded me with a giggle. "Here's a tractor."

I took the toy—this one metal instead of plastic—and ran my hands over it. Then I drove it back and forth a few times. "Is it a John Deere?"

"No, silly!" Bette reproached. "It's not green! It's red. It's a Maxxum, like Grandpa's."

"Honey," Derek reminded his daughter, "Mike can't tell green from red. He's color blind."

Another giggle from Bette.

Then her toddling sister swept through the farm like a tornado.

"Daddy!" Bette whined as she jumped to her feet. "Daddy, spank her! Why does Polly always have to ruin everything?"

As Derek scooped up the perpetrator, he asked lightly, "See there, Mike, don't you want a whole houseful of these little nippers?"

Just when we had repaired the farmstead, Tish called us to the table. The meal was worth the wait. I asked, "Derek, do you eat this well all the time?"

"I'm telling you, man, you need to get married. It beats cooking for yourself."

With a smirk, I asked, "Is that why a guy gets married?"

Tish tousled my hair. "Little pitchers, Mike."

I grinned. "Tish, I meant that he shouldn't expect you to cook just because you're the wife."

She chortled. "Yeah. Right. But if we had to eat his cooking, we'd all die. So I don't mind taking one for the team."

Then her voice suddenly switched to a hard matronly tone. "Now, what's with you two not shaving?"

Yesterday when we had made a pact to grow beards, Derek had made me promise to stay strong and back him with his wife. He didn't know what she would think of

291

facial hair, but for some reason, he thought she might not approve.

"Winter's right around the corner," I explained. "And you know how balaclavas get all soggy and damp. You run twenty miles with that stuff rubbing on you, and you end up with a raw face."

She wasn't convinced. "Mike, you don't need a balaclava. You can just wear a big stocking cap over your whole head."

"True," I admitted. "In fact, that's almost exactly what I wear. It freaks people out when they see me, but when it's really cold, I wear a specially made mask that has a nose hole but no eye holes."

"What color is it?" she asked.

Derek cracked up. Then I lost it. We were a hopeless case of giggles for the next ten minutes.

By dessert, the two youngest kids were fussing, so Tish excused herself to put them to bed. Bette climbed into my lap and pulled the phone from my inner jacket pocket.

"Bette," Derek snapped, "put that back."

"It's okay," I said, breaking into a smile.

A few seconds later, she announced, "It's okay, Daddy. He showed us how it works." But a moment later, she declared, "It's broken."

"No kidding?" I gasped.

With a grin on his face, Derek said, "What makes you think it's broken?"

"Because it won't come on," she reasoned.

I held my finger on the screen until my dad's voice said, "Read mail."

After I tapped it, it began listing emails beginning from the most recent.

"Oh!" the delighted girl bubbled. "That's how it talked yesterday at school. But the light is broken."

I slid my finger down the screen until Dad said, "Settings." Tapped. Found the icon for Screen. Tapped. Found the icon for Brightness. Tapped.

"Voila," I said as I handed it back to her.

"Oh," she said again. "It's just like your phone, Daddy. Except it talks!"

I explained that it was my dad talking. Bette was intrigued.

All three of us moved to the garage where Derek wanted to install a new plastic liner on his bumper. Tish had apparently parked too close to a concrete barrier and had torn the old one. From under a tool bench near the wall, he pulled a rolling chair and parked it next to where he would be working. Patting it, he said, "Have a seat."

After investigating the device, I eased my weight onto it. "Is this designed to hold your tool box so you can roll it around to where you are working?"

"Yep," he said as he lay on his back on the concrete floor and slid under the front of the minivan. "Bette, can you hand me that little plastic bag there?"

"This one?" she asked.

"That's right. Thank you."

He fiddled with the bag for a minute, and then he handed it back. "Can you open it, Sweetie?"

Her little hands were no match for the tough plastic. "I can't get it, Daddy. I'm sorry!"

"Here," I held out my hand. From the pocket of my jeans, I pulled a small folding knife. A second later, I handed the open bag back to her. "Don't spill it. It has some little gizmos in it."

"What's a gizmo?" she inquired.

"A thing-a-ma-bob," I answered seriously. "Also known as a whatcha-ma-call-it."

She giggled and began telling me about the Christmas tree they were going to set up next week after Thanksgiving.

Derek hit his knuckles and grunted.

Bette asked me what I wanted for Christmas, but I recognized the ploy and asked her what *she* wanted. The list was long. She was nowhere near the end of it when I heard a muffled curse from under the bumper.

"Problems in paradise?" I asked.

For reply, he rasped, "Honey, could you hand Daddy that flashlight? I can't quite see this stupid thing."

"Daddy, you aren't supposed to use the S-word," his daughter chided as she handed him the light.

"Thank you."

"Find it yet?" I asked.

"It isn't lost. It's just that I have to snap in this plastic thinga—what did you call it? Gizmo. I have to snap in this plastic gizmo, but I have to put it through the metal part of the bumper and into the plastic new part. And I can't see up in there."

"Let Uncle Mike do it," Bette suggested.

"Yeah, right," he scoffed. But a moment later, he invited me to join him on the floor. When I was beside him, he guided my hand into the interior curve of the bumper. "You feel that hole?"

"Yep," I answered.

Then he handed me the little connector gizmo and explained how it should be installed. "You think you can guide it in there? Because I can't see it."

Snap.

Disgusted, he asked, "Did you just snap that damn thing in there?"

"Daddy! Don't cuss!"

"I did," I acknowledged. "Isn't that what I was supposed to do?"

"Son of a—" He left off the last part in deference to his daughter. Probably because he didn't want her to report on his naughty utterances. After letting out a long breath, he said, "Good. Thanks. Next time this thing is due for an oil change, I'll just bring it over for you."

"Okay," I said as I got to my feet and slapped the dust off my back.

He muttered, "How the devil did you do that so fast? That's talent, man."

"Sure," I agreed "But I don't know what color shirt I'm wearing."

"It's blue," Bette supplied.

I held out my hand for a high five. "Good. I think blue is my favorite color. It's the color of the sky, right?"

Skeptically, the girl asked, "Did someone tell you that?"

Holding back a laugh, I replied, "Yes. Someone did tell me that."

"You can do things other people can't do," Bette reminded me.

I nodded. "That's true. Not very many. But sometimes I can help sighted people. Like when they can't see the gizmo in the bumper. Or when they have to get out of an airplane in the dark."

I let myself into Everly's house—her uncle's house—and called out. No answer. She was still at choir practice. This month, she was off the hook for playing piano, and another accompanist had taken over. I suspected the congregation was glad to be rid of the flamboyant blind guy accompanying their hymns with jazz improv.

Okay with me.

Hoping to wash out any excess beer from my system, I headed to the kitchen sink for a glass of water. I should've headed a little more slowly.

As nearly as I could later dissect the chain of events, I first hit the open dishwasher door with my shin. That caused me to topple face first into the edge of the countertop. Then I fell down onto the dishwasher door, striking it with my abdomen, and catching my shirt on something. With a ripping sound as the fabric gave way, I bounced off the door and crashed toward the floor. The back of my head connected solidly with the perpendicular cabinet.

Dazed, I reached upward and found the offending dishwasher door just above my face. I tried pushing it upward, but the heavily laden lower rack must have been resting on it. After shoving the rack into the machine, I again slammed the door upward. It didn't latch. So I rammed my palm against it until it did.

Coming up to my knees, I leaned against the cabinet for several minutes, shivering and trying to catch my breath. Finally, I drew my left foot under me, but when I tried to put my weight on it, it slid to the side. Something had made the floor slippery.

Breath ragged, I fumbled for my phone. In a few seconds, Derek answered, "Yo?"

"Derek, it's Mike."

"Yeah, I figured that when my phone said it was you. What's up? You miss me already?"

"I fell and smacked my head."

Sometimes a person's voice says, "Hey, when you get a minute, could you give me a hand?" And sometimes it says, "Help!"

Mine must have said the latter because he hastily replied, "I'm on my way."

When he walked in a few minutes later, I was still kneeling and leaning against the cabinet.

"Holy shit!" he emoted. "It looks like somebody slaughtered a sheep in here! My god, did you sacrifice one of Everly's dogs on an altar? There's blood everywhere." He whipped the hand towel from the oven door handle.

Folding it, he said, "Here, take this with your left hand. Hold it on your face."

With a shaking hand, I took the towel and did as instructed and mumbled, "The only thing I sacrificed was my face."

"Now give me your right hand. We better get you down to the ER. I think that's gonna need some stitches."

I heard the front door open again and Everly's solid steps crossed the living room and stopped at the doorway to the kitchen. "Oh, my god! Mike!" she squawked. "Why would someone even bother trying to kill you? You're doing a pretty good job of it all by yourself."

"You left the dishwasher door open again," I grumbled as I came to my feet with Derek's assistance. "And while I find it flattering that you sometimes forget I'm blind, let me just inform you: I'm blind."

At the instant I stood upright, everything lurched sideways and I went down again.

Derek made a startled noise. Everly grabbed my other arm to steady me. Sounding calmer now, she told Derek, "He needs extra support when he's light-headed. Fewer environmental cues."

Everly sent Derek home once I was buckled into the passenger seat of her pickup. I managed not to vomit until I stepped out onto the concrete drive at the emergency room. I was glad Derek wasn't there to see me lose the nice dinner his wife had prepared.

Sixteen stitches later, Everly drove me home. She waited outside the bathroom door while I brushed my teeth. Then she tucked me in and bid me a good night.

Five hours later, I was sitting on the couch in the living room. My cheek was throbbing. My head was pounding. My brain was churning over the depositions I'd been listening to in the Stoltz case.

297

I heard a slight noise. Probably one of the cats sashaying around.

Then I heard a light switch and simultaneous metallic click that sounded a lot like a round being chambered in a handgun.

My eyes flew open and my jaw dropped. I was certain I was about to be shot to death.

Before I even had a chance to dive sideways off the couch, Everly snapped, "What the hell are you doing sitting here in the dark?"

As I fought down my racing heart and resulting nausea, I bleated, "Were you planning on shooting me?"

She took a couple deep breaths and popped the cartridge free of the chamber. "Trouble sleeping? Headache?"

"Yes and yes. And wondering what to do about Dolores Stoltz and her sexual harassment circus."

Everly dropped on the couch beside me and put her arm over my shoulders. In a soothing voice, she said, "Dear Heavenly Father, please be with your son Mike. Help him remember that there are those who care for him so deeply. Those who support him no matter what. Help him know that the physical pain he feels now will ease soon. And give him your guidance, dear God, to keep him on the right path. In the name of your holy son, Jesus Christ our lord. Amen."

I swallowed a lump in my throat and rubbed a hand across my burning eyes.

Her voice sounded as kind as I had ever heard it when she offered, "Now go get some sleep. Let me give you a hand."

I couldn't move.

"Come on," she prompted.

I took in a ragged breath. All I could manage to say was, "Everly, no one has ever prayed for me. Ever."

"You're wrong about that," she said as she pulled me to my feet.

With my arm over her shoulder, I let her lead me down the hallway. Just as we approached the bed, I said, "May I ask you a question?"

"I'm not going to bed with you," she resolved tiredly.

"What color is Honu? Is he a bay?"

"Sorrel," she replied. "Why do you ask?"

I frowned. "I know what a bay is."

She informed me, "A sorrel is the same red body color as a bay. But they have red points instead of black."

"Points," I said. "Mane and tail."

She sighed. "Right. Go to sleep."

Chapter Twelve

⠠⠄⠄ ⠏⠢⠹ ⠀⠄⠹⠡⠒⠊ ⠇⠄

During my first cup of coffee, Derek called.

I answered, "What's up?"

"Don't come outside until I get there," he advised.

"I'm all right," I said. "Everly prayed for me last night. I'm healing miraculously fast."

"Okay. Whatever. But it's raining. So don't go outside until I get there. Okay?"

"Great!" I said. And I meant it. "I love running in the rain."

Voice heavy with irony, he said, "It's twenty-eight degrees. You ain't gonna like running in this rain. There's a glare of ice on everything. So Gunnar wants us indoors today. Since my knee's been bothering me, he wants me on the exercise bike. You'll be on the high-speed treadmill if you're up to it."

"I'm up to it," I said. "But I'm not happy about it."

Immediately after he disconnected, I got another call. Though it wasn't a computer-generated voice, it sounded like one.

"Is this Michael Sandsebrotsky?" a female asked.

"Yes, it is."

"I am the CMO for the case involving yourself and Luther Dobson. Are you familiar with this case?"

300

"Yes," I replied. "What is a CMO?"

"Case management officer. I am calling to inform you," she sounded mechanical and extremely bored, "that Mr. Dobson failed to show at his court appearance."

I waited for more. Seemingly, she was finished. "And so what does that mean?"

"It means Mr. Dobson didn't appear for his court appearance," she answered simply.

With a sigh, I thanked her for her time. Then I texted Dad and relayed the news to him. As I sat processing the information, Everly set a pile of laundry in front of me.

"I sewed tags in the back of all your shorts and sweats."

"You did?"

"Yeah. I hope it helps."

"It will," I assured her. "Thank you."

Before she could reply, Derek knocked on the door.

Feeling like an infirm old-age patient, I was led off the porch with Everly on one arm and Derek on the other. "This is a little too much fuss," I lamented.

Then, despite all their assistance, I fell on my butt, taking Everly with me. "Holy cats!" I emoted. "This is just like a skating rink."

"No kidding," she replied dryly. "Do you know how to skate?"

"Sure," I said. "We used to go speed skating on a frozen lake up in the mountains."

"Speed skating?" Derek asked with a chuckle.

"Yeah!" I replied enthusiastically. "Dad thought I was going forty miles an hour one time!"

"How many stitches did you get for that?" Everly responded.

"Very droll," I returned.

I had never been on a high-speed treadmill. After Gunnar examined Derek's knee and gave him instructions for the stationary bike, he led me to the appliance.

He explained, "This thing is designed for horses. The belt surface is five feet wide and twelve feet long. There are steel bars on the sides and in the front so you won't have trouble staying on the track. I'm going to fix a bungee cord across near the back so if you hit it, you know you have to move up. Right?"

"Sure," I said, disappointed with being back on the treadmill. But I knew running on the rink outdoors would be less fun. And infinitely more dangerous.

As Gunnar moved to the settings on the machine, he said, "It's supposed to be in the fifties tomorrow. So it'll be muddy. But not slick. So you guys plan to start running tomorrow in late morning. And run on the paved streets in town. That track between here and Ev's place will be muck."

He started the treadmill. It took no time at all to get accustomed to it.

After a few minutes, Gunnar asked, "Mike? How is it?"

"Great," I grinned. "Way better than a regular treadmill."

"Good." He started to move away, but then he turned toward me again. "Mike, I want to explain something to you. When I told you before that you run like a duck, I didn't mean it was really noticeable to anyone else. If I didn't know beans from bull-puckey about running, I don't think I'd know you were blind from watching you run. But running is the only thing I do know. And I knew the first time I watched a video of one of your races that something was different. It isn't totally because you're blind. You flopped that arm across your chest. Lots of sighted runners do that. And you tipped your head back too far. Lots of sighted runners do that, too. So I don't want you to be self-conscious about any of that stuff. Okay?"

"Okay."

302

From the bike, Derek said one of the only serious things of that day. "And you don't do any of that stuff now anyway."

Fifteen minutes later, Gunnar returned. "Mike, I'm gonna turn off the treadmill."

"Okay," I said. I had thought I would be putting on some serious miles. Apparently not.

The belt slowed and stopped. I ducked under the steel bar that constituted the side rail. "Why am I stopping so soon?"

"Here," Gunnar said. "Take this; I'm handing you a towel. Your face is bleeding. I think maybe some of the stitches came out. You're done for the day."

Shelley fed us lunch. Derek drove me home and made sure I got inside without breaking any bones. Before he turned to go, I said, "Hey, could you help me with something?"

"Sure. What do you need?"

"I need you to help me commit a felony. Do you have your laptop with you?" I inquired.

He laughed. "Felony, huh? Sounds like fun. I do have a computer in the car. But I'll risk all my bones if I go back out there. Why do you need it?"

"I have a movie for you to watch. Go get your computer."

By the time he returned from his careful trip on the ice, I had prepared two mugs of hot chocolate. As his computer booted up, I asked him to accompany me to the master bedroom.

"This isn't going to be kinky, is it?" he posited.

"Depends what you plan to do with a thumb drive." We were standing now in Everly's room. "Do you see her laptop?"

"Yeah. It's on the night stand," he replied.

"Is there a thumb drive?"

He crossed the room. "Yep. You want me to grab it?"

I thought about that for a moment. Then I stepped toward him. "You tell me where it is. I'll pick it up. Then maybe only one of us will go to prison."

He laughed again and complied. "Just what kind of top secret stuff is on this thing anyway?"

"A few nights ago, I made a late night trip to the john. Everly was on the phone. I caught enough to suspect she was talking to her superior at the FBI. They were discussing some kind of evidence. When I got back to my room, I stood just inside the door and listened until she hung up. Then she pulled out a thumb drive and closed her computer. I figured the computer was password protected, but maybe not the USB."

In the kitchen, I stuck the USB into Derek's computer. It took us a while to find what I wanted him to watch and interpret: video surveillance at the airport before the bombed flight took off.

The first view of the waiting area at the gate had been taken from behind me. Derek described every detail. While we were pulling up the second video, he said, "Hey, maybe I could get a job someday providing audio description for the visually impaired."

"If you keep working at it, you may just become proficient," I agreed. He smacked my shoulder.

The second video came on. Derek again provided play-by-play.

"Okay. There you come with your hand on the ticket agent's shoulder."

"Is she cute?" I asked.

He guffawed. "If you like big girls. I'd say she'd clock in at a good two-eighty. I guess color wouldn't matter to you."

"She was black," I recalled. "Great sense of humor. Good grammar. Nice lady."

"How did you know she was black? Just from the way she talked?"

"She didn't speak ebonics, if that's what you mean. She had a velvety voice. Deep and sensuous. I've never heard a white woman talk like that. And I could tell by her smell. Is the other guy there yet?"

"Nope. Just you sitting there having a talk with your phone. You can smell a black person?"

"I had a friend in college who worked at Disneyland in the summer. He said white people smell like wet dogs when it rains. What's going on?" I indicated the computer screen.

"You're still talking to your phone."

"And holding it in my left hand a few inches above my chest."

"Right," he agreed. "Here he comes. God, that's a freaking ugly dog. Holy crap! I'd shoot that thing just to do it a favor."

I snickered. "What breed is it?"

"It looks like a chow crossed with an ugly 70s shag rug. It's covered with mats. God, you just know from looking at that thing that it smells like a sewer."

"It didn't smell like roses," I recalled.

He chortled. "I bet that ugly bugger shits pure hair. It keeps digging at itself."

"Hair in the feces?" I mused. "That explains something."

"I haven't seen too many guide dogs," Derek stated, "but I'll bet they're usually clean and brushed."

I agreed. "Labs and German shepherds have low maintenance coats. That's one of the reasons they're used for guide work."

A moment later, Derek asked, "You sure you weren't talking to this dude?"

305

"I'm sure," I stated. "If I had spoken with him, I would recall his voice, and I don't."

He sounded skeptical when he said, "He's a good actor, then. Sure looks like he's having a confab with you. He talks then you start talking, and he looks like you're telling him off or something."

"Is he blind?" I asked.

"Looks like it," he replied.

I let him think about my question for a moment.

After a full minute, he said, "I'm going to back it up and watch part of it again. You asked me that on purpose, didn't you?"

"Right. You've been around me long enough to know I do some things differently than a sighted person. If he was born sighted, he'd have sighted mannerisms. But if he was born blind, you'll recognize it. What do you think?"

He was quiet for several minutes. The clicks told me he was watching parts of the video repeatedly.

"Oh, shoot," he muttered. "Crap. That idiot is no blinder than I am." He was quiet again for a full minute. "Okay, here is the stewardess."

"Flight attendant," I corrected.

"Oh, shut up. Can you quit being politically correct for one minute while I figure out whether you bombed your flight? Okay, you picked up your backpack. She carried your other bag."

"I didn't have another bag," I said.

"A cloth bag?" he offered. "With a drawstring?"

I shook my head. "Nope. Just the backpack."

He muttered another curse and replayed the video yet again. "Son of a—! That lousy SOB. The guy pretending to be blind came in with that drawstring bag and set it next to your left foot. When she took you, she picked up that bag. Shit! You think they were working together?"

"Maybe," I said. "And I think your expletive is exactly what was in the drawstring bag. What happened to him after I left?"

"He's still sitting there. . . Still sitting. . . still—nope, there he goes. He just left the screen. Can't tell where he went."

Wearing a scowl, I asked, "How is he walking with the dog? I mean, does it look like the dog is pulling forward on the harness, or does it look like the man is leading the dog?"

Derek went back again and watched the man leaving the gate area. Then he backed it up to when the man had entered the video. With a muffled curse of frustration, he pulled up another video and watched the man go through security. "I don't get what you're asking."

I explained how a guide dog is trained to pull forward and keep its handler moving in a straight line. "The dog doesn't understand things like 'Take me downtown to the mall' or 'Find a Starbucks'. They can find a counter or a door or a chair on command. They move left, right, forward, or halt on command. But they don't do complicated maneuvers. Does any of that help you recognize whether this guy is a phony?"

"Boy, I don't know," Derek lamented. "I'd have to know what the hell I'm looking for to know if he's—hey! Wait a second. Son of a bitch."

"Your daughter is going to be mad when I tell her what a potty mouth you've become," I warned.

Ignoring me, he became excited. "He's pulling the dog. Definitely pulling the dog, not the other way around."

Suddenly an idea came to me. "Is all of the airport video footage on that drive?"

He fiddled with the keys for a moment. "Maybe. Anything in particular?"

"The pet relief area," I suggested just as Everly came in the back door.

"Hi, Roomie," I said glibly.

I heard Derek swallow hard.

"Hey, guys. Short workout today?" She began peeling off her boots and layers of coats.

"Yeah," I answered. "Derek has a bum knee, and I have a bum face."

There was a long moment of silence. Then Everly stepped farther into the room and, her voice low and ominous, asked, "What are you doing?"

I spoke up. "Derek is being my eyes, so I can figure out who tried to kill me in the plane. Can you help us find the video of the pet relief area?"

Derek asked, "What exactly is a pet relief area?"

"Usually," I explained, "it is a square piece of plastic turf, maybe four by four feet, with a plastic fire hydrant or something."

She crossed the room and yanked the thumb drive from Derek's computer.

I stood and held up a conciliatory hand. "Everly, I think I know how the explosive got into the airport. It was in the dog."

"The security folks swabbed the dog harness and leash for traces of explosive," she snapped. "It was clean."

"I know," I said.

Before I could elaborate, Derek threw in dryly, "You don't say? They practically washed the damned harness with swabs. I'm surprised they didn't take it off and submerge it."

"They can't," I broke in. "They never take off the harness. When I go through security with my dog, I hand them the leash, then I go through the metal detector while they swab the harness."

To Everly, Derek probed, "That other dog smelled the explosives, didn't it?"

"What other dog?" I asked.

Everly answered begrudgingly, "Yeah. The bomb dog was alerting. But it was alerting at the other dog's butt. Not unusual for a dog. But the handler missed it."

"Which handler?" I asked.

She turned toward me. "What?"

"Anybody who handles a dog is a handler. The guide dog has a handler. The bomb dog has a handler."

"I was talking about the bomb dog," Everly clarified.

"I'm suggesting that the explosive was *in* the dog," I reiterated. "It was packed in plastic sealable bags, maybe. What if the alleged blind guy took the dog to the pet relief area and let it dump out the explosives. He uses a plastic bag to seal up the proceeds—and the smell— and slips it into the drawstring bag. Then the flight attendant picks it up when she takes me into the plane. She told me the flight would be packed, so she wanted to stow my backpack up front. So what if—after she seated me—she opened the drawstring bag, pulled out the dog poop and explosive cocktail, assembled her components, and put the finished bomb back in my backpack."

Everly didn't say anything.

"That would explain why I smelled dog poop before the flight," I reminded her. "And why I smelled burning hair right before impact. Derek said the dog was covered with hair mats and was biting itself. Its poop was probably full of hair. That means the bomb was, too."

Derek threw in his two cents worth. "Pacino, if you've watched the video, you know the guy with the chow isn't really blind. Right?"

"What are you talking about?" she asked. She still sounded mad. But at least she was expressing interest in the cause and not just in busting us amateur sleuths.

Derek asked her to give him the USB. She hesitated. He demanded, "Do you want to see what I'm looking at or not?"

With an exasperated sigh, she handed it to him. A few long, silent minutes later, he said, "See?"

"Back it up," she suggested.

Then she mumbled, "Son of a bitch."

I chortled. "That's exactly what he said. What's going on? Descriptive audio for the visually impaired, please."

"The guy looks up and nods at her," Derek explained.

"I can nod," I argued.

Everly said, "You can't nod in response to a shrug twenty feet away in a busy airport terminal."

I thought about that. "Nope. Probably not."

"Okay," Everly posed as she pulled out a chair and dropped onto it. "So what else have you dolts discovered?"

"Can you find the video for the pet relief area?" I asked.

It took her a while to find the correct surveillance. But I could tell as the other two watched the silent footage that my theory was plausible.

"And it's definitely not a guide dog," Derek pointed out. He pulled up the video of the imposter walking with the dog and repeated my guide dog explanations.

Pulling the thumb drive from Derek's computer, Everly wordlessly walked into her room and closed the door.

"You think we just broke her case for her?" Derek asked quietly.

I sighed. "I hope so. Did you recognize the fake blind guy or the flight attendant?"

"The stewardess, you mean? Nope. Neither of them. But as I think of it, he was wearing a disguise. He had on a hat with bushy hair that was probably fake. And he had huge dark wraparound glasses. Trench coat. And that dog was way too ugly to be a guide dog."

"I've never heard of a chow as a guide dog," I surmised. "Labs.   German   shepherds.   Golden   retrievers. Labradoodles. But chows just aren't suited for that kind of work. As far as that goes, I don't know what they are suited for."

"I think they're a main ingredient in some kind of Chinese dish." With a grimace, Derek stated, "Maybe good for target practice. First dog that ever attacked me when I was running was a damned chow."

"There's another thing we have in common."

Everly was still in her room on the phone when Derek left. King Kamehameha slunk onto my lap and slept while I lay on the couch listening to my phone speed-read the Gospel of Luke.

When Everly emerged, she stood still for a moment and finally asked, "What are you listening to? And how can you understand it that fast?"

I told her what it was. "Once you get used to it, you can turn up the speed. It's also good training for understanding teenagers, all of whom speak at two and a half times the speed of sound."

"Why aren't you reading your Braille Bible?"

"Head hurts," I moaned. "It's easier to listen than to move."

As she went into the kitchen, she called over her shoulder, "Stick with the gospels first. Leave Revelation for last. Or for never. It's weird."

Out of curiosity, I pulled up the Book of Revelation on my phone. With all the numbers and diadems and multi-headed monsters, it read more like something from the Iliad than anything I would have expected from scriptures. Calling to her in the kitchen, I said, "You're right. I'll stick with Luke for now."

Four miles into our run on the wet local streets, Derek said, "I sure wish you weren't such a charming son-of-a-bitch."

I busted up laughing.

"I mean it," he said, though I could tell from his tone that he didn't. "Last night, I'm sitting in my recliner watching a soccer game, and Shelley comes by to drop off some cupcakes she made for the kids."

"For the kids?" I plied. "How many of them did you polish off?"

"Only seven. But don't tell anyone. So, Shelley is sitting there jaw-jacking with my wife, and she says something about how cute you are."

I laughed again.

"Then my wife has the audacity to agree with her. They went on and on about how much they like your handsome smile."

"Really?" I asked without humor. "Kimberlyn says my smile is weird."

"Kimberlyn is weird. Buddy, do yourself a favor and punt her," Derek muttered. "But here's the rest of the story. I mentioned that you had done some modeling. So Tish looks you up online and finds your modeling agency, and they sit there and ogle your portfolio."

I grinned. "You're kidding! I haven't done any modeling for years. My portfolio is still up?"

"Hell, the company that peddles five hundred dollar sunglasses is still using your ugly mug."

I scowled. "That's interesting. The company that peddles five hundred dollar sunglasses hasn't sent me a check for a very long time. I better look into the matter."

He guffawed. "As a thanks for bringing this to your attention, I believe you should take me with you on the trip to the Bahamas that you'll be able to afford on the proceeds of your inquiry."

"You don't understand how models get paid," I remarked dryly. "The proceeds will get us exactly two miles out of town."

"Are you telling me you got paid more to be head referee at the Solomon, California, Public School District than you did being photographed in five hundred dollar sunglasses?"

"Bingo."

Two days before the marathon Derek and I were scheduled to run in Montana, I got a call from Kimberlyn. Claiming she was ashamed of her behavior, she begged me to forgive her and invited me to her home for dinner that evening.

On the one hand, I felt that I should—as Derek had suggested—punt her. On the other hand—as Derek would have recognized—I was lonely.

When she pulled up, I put my hand on top of the passenger door and remarked, "New car?"

"Yeah!" she chirped. "You like it?"

"Nice," I relayed. Stepping inside and sweeping my hand across the dash before I remembered that she thought I moved my hands weirdly, I said, "This is really nice."

Really expensive, I reflected to myself.

And electric.

At her place, she led me to the kitchen and plunked me on a chair. While she alternately stirred something and chopped something else and fixed me a drink, she rattled on about her second grade class. They had made Christmas decorations to take home.

"Here you go. I hope you like it. This is a recipe I picked up in Acapulco last year." She handed me a glass and waited while I tasted it.

At first sip, it wasn't too bad. But there was some kind of aftertaste that reminded me of furniture polish. I conjured up a smile. "Thanks."

313

"You like it?" she asked expectantly.

"Great," I lied. "What are you cooking over there?"

"Oh, just some pasta and salad. Is that okay for you?"

"Absolutely," I said. "What are your plans for the holidays?" I took another sip of the drink, hoping it had improved. It hadn't.

"I'm going to the Caribbean!" she emoted. "One of those all-inclusive resorts, you know? The kind where you can drink all you want and eat all you want. You just can't leave the resort because the locals are really poor blacks and they mug tourists. But it's really nice! They have eleven restaurants on site, and there's a swim-up bar in the pool, and waiters deliver drinks to your chair on the beach. I can't wait!"

"Sounds great. How long will you be there?"

"I'm flying out the day after school is out and getting a sub to fill in for me for a couple days at the end of break."

"Is your family going?" I asked.

"No, it's—" she stopped abruptly. Then she resumed. "Sorry, I was trying to cut this carrot without slicing my finger. I'm going with some friends from college. How about you? Are you going to California?"

"Yes. I'm flying out on Christmas Eve." I swallowed. Swallowed again. Felt suddenly nauseous. Took a deep breath. Then another.

Getting to my feet, I said, "Kimberlyn, thanks for the invitation. But I'm going home now."

"What?" she blurted. "But, you can't. Finish your drink! I'll have dinner ready in a little while. You can't leave yet."

Vigorously, I rubbed a hand on my face. Then I snapped open my cane and made my way to the front door.

She trotted after me. "But I can't drive you right now. I have stuff on the stove. It'll burn."

"I'll walk." Firmly closing the door behind me to keep her from following, I staggered down the sidewalk as fast as I could manage without vomiting. I calculated it was almost three quarters of a mile to Everly's. The cold night air felt good on my clammy skin. In fact, the farther I walked, the better I felt.

By the time I left the city limits where the footing turned from pavement to sand, my stomach was starting to settle down. When I entered the living room, Everly looked up. Startled, she asked, "Why are you back so soon?"

Folding the cane and hooking it on a belt loop on my jeans, I dropped onto the sofa and said, "You don't suppose Kimberlyn would poison someone, do you?"

I was met with absolute silence.

Shaking my head, I said, "I suppose not. But she made me a drink that tasted like floor wax. And within minutes, I thought I was going to be sick."

"You're serious?" she probed.

"Serious," I said as I flopped down on the couch. Unfortunately, one of the cats was already occupying the couch. He/she was not happy with my intrusion.

Everly crossed toward me and put a hand on my forehead. "Do you need to see a doctor?"

"I don't think so. It was nip and tuck there for a while. But I have lost the desire to barf. Fortunately, I heal fast."

She stood uncertainly for a long time. Then she said, "Let's go."

We ended up back in my old haunts. The emergency room. Everly insisted they take blood samples. Then she disappeared for an hour during which time I was thoroughly bored. And beginning to get more than a little hungry.

When she finally returned, she led me outside to her pickup. On the way back to the house, she said, "Mike, I don't think I can protect you here anymore."

I absorbed that for a while. "Where else would I go? I mean, what happens if I keep running away from life and then there are no more somewhere elses to hide?"

She sighed. "I arrested Kimberlyn. She admitted she tried to poison you. She did not admit who put a hundred thousand dollars in her bank account two days ago. But she will eventually."

I turned my face toward her. "What did you say?"

"Mike, someone paid her."

"To kill me?" I squawked.

"She said she wasn't trying to kill you."

"Then what? Was she trying to polish my insides?"

Everly said, "We'll find out what's going on. She swore she wasn't trying to kill you. Maybe she just has a screw loose."

I pondered that for a while. Then I asked, "What about Charles? He could afford to supply her with a new car and a fancy vacation."

"Remember the Zana Kazemi I found on the terrorist top ten list?"

I answered, "Every other minute of every waking hour. But it's a different guy, right? You said the real bad guy was younger than Charles."

"About thirty, give or take a couple years. By the time he made his first attack, Charles was established in Solomon as an ophthalmologist and attending dance recitals and his kids' softball games."

Derek and I didn't leave Everly's house the following morning until she had given him an update. And a warning to keep his eyes open.

As soon as we were out the yard gate, he said softly, "Someone wants to slow you down."

"What?"

"Think about it," he pointed out. "Everything that happens to you happens a day or two before a race."

I thought about that for a few strides. "I fell on the dishwasher door a couple weeks ago."

"That was your own fault," he reminded me.

"It was Everly's fault," I amended.

"When did your dog die? I mean, was it right before a race?"

I thought about that. "It was two days before a marathon."

"What about the plane crash?"

"You're wrong there. That one was a couple weeks before. But I don't think downing a commercial plane was meant to just slow me down. That would have been meant to stop me. Permanently."

"Okay, how about the guy standing in your house? The one the cops shot?"

"Two days before a race," I said, realizing he might be onto something.

"And here we are. The day before a race, and you're suffering from floor polish hangover."

I shook my head. "But the raft shooting was between races."

"Okay," he reasoned, "so between races, someone tries to kill you. Two days before, they just try to distract you."

I scowled. "That's nuts."

He shrugged. "Yeah. You're right. I'm trying, here, man. It's the best I could come up with."

Chapter Thirteen

The weather in Montana was what one might politely call a wintery mix. In less polite circles, it was crap.

The nearby ski resort was filled with happy people as the slopes received several inches of powder. But down in the basin where we would run, it was ugly. Wet, heavy snow was punctuated with occasional bouts of sleet and rain. The wind was steady at fifteen to twenty miles an hour. Temperatures hovered in the mid-thirties.

Having adjusted our tether so neither of us had to hold anything in our gloved hands, we bounced at the starting line until the gun fired.

We followed Paul Stuebbens for the first fifteen miles. Just like usual. He stayed beside us for the next mile. Just before we pulled away, he spoke the only words any of us uttered in that time.

"Saw you on TV last Sunday morning. Did you really get fired for raping that woman, Mike?"

Instantly, Derek said, "Don't kill him, Mike."

I didn't kill Paul. But I telepathically sent ill wishes his way.

I shouldn't have let Paul Stuebbens get under my skin. But I had. And Derek knew it. We hadn't run hundreds of

318

miles together without developing a sense of the other's thoughts and moods.

Instead of telling me not to worry about Paul— and thereby reinforcing Paul in my mind— Derek said, "One more week."

For the next half mile, I pondered what he was talking about. One more week to what? Then I remembered. Tish's due date was next week.

"Boy or girl?" I asked.

"Don't know. We're going to find out the old fashioned way," he replied.

He succeeded in keeping my thoughts focused on his impending child for about two minutes. Then I was back to the Stoltz case, though I knew I should be focusing on the race.

Dolores Stoltz. . . what a dingbat. Prince Taylor— who hadn't previously struck me as being a creep of a lawyer— had apparently talked her into taking a tour on the media whirlwind.

Which led me again to the question: Who was paying him?

That thought nagged at me. It nagged at my feet, too. I wanted to go faster.

A hundred thousand dollars. New electric car. All inclusive Caribbean vacation. Who had paid Kimberlyn?

Once, Derek gave a slight tug on the tether. "Mind your pace. You're letting your brain take over. Listen to your feet."

I tried to take his advice. We were right behind the pace vehicle now. The pavement had proved to be level. No potholes. No unevenness. With a few seconds' rumination, I reached down and unclipped the tether.

And left Derek.

It seemed to take the driver of the pacer a few seconds to realize I had broken free. When my knee barely ticked the back bumper, I reached down and slammed my hand against the trunk twice.

He got the message and sped up.

So did I.

My feet pounded out my raging frustration. Frustration with all of it. Murdered guide dog. Plane crash. Stoltz case. Home intruder. Murdered river guide. Furniture polish. All of it.

I continued speeding up until Mile Twenty-Five.

Then I was afraid I had broken the cardinal rule of distance racing: even paces win long races.

My lungs were on fire. My legs were jelly. My arms and shoulders ached. It seems odd to a lot of non-runners, but arms are often the most tired part of the body by the end of a marathon.

I gutted through the last bit of the race. I knew I was slowing, but I didn't want to give my body the satisfaction. So I pushed harder.

I heard the finish line. Not the line itself, of course, but the flurry of activity there. I no longer felt connected to my body. It was like I was hovering somewhere above the scene.

Legs on autopilot, lungs burning like a blow torch, heart feeling like someone was stabbing it with an ice pick, I heard Gunnar's voice telling me I was across.

Then I crumpled. My legs cramped. Arms cramped. Abdomen cramped. Back cramped. Neck cramped. My chin slammed into the wet, cold pavement. I could hear voices around me but no words. I could feel people tugging me and pulling me. But all I could do was gasp for air and retch.

Drama.

This was the kind of drama Paul Stuebbens imparted at the end of every race. I vaguely wondered if it was his medical team tending to me.

But I didn't care.

Somewhere along the line, though, it occurred to me that Gunnar was going to kill me. I had broken protocol. I had run off without Derek. I had ignored the pace Gunnar had fought so diligently to implant in my legs, my lungs, my heart, and my head.

I had let him down.

He would fire me.

Then I would be without a school. Without a coach. Without a woman.

There suddenly seemed to be a lot of excitement. I was moving fast, rolling through a hospital corridor. There were anxious voices around me. A lot of voices. All talking at once. All seemingly frantic.

Then one voice overshadowed the rest and said something that seemed totally incongruous to me.

"He bit his tongue. Okay? Did you hear me? His tongue is bleeding."

Indeed, my tongue hurt. So did my jaw. So did every muscle in my body.

I tried to sit up. Too many hands pushed me down. Someone asked if I had a history of ulcers. No, I answered.

I asked for a drink. Someone started feeding me ice chips. Eventually, I was given a sports drink. I downed the slightly bitter, slightly salty brew and asked for more.

A woman said, "You were vomiting blood. We thought you had a bleeding ulcer. You just about got hauled into the OR to have your belly opened up."

"What?" I muttered.

"But you bit your tongue. That's where the blood was coming from. Not from your stomach. Is your tongue sore?"

"Everything's sore," I rasped.

Then Gunnar was there.

I dreaded this. He was going to read me the riot act, and I would be lucky to still have a position with him after the stunt I pulled and the drama at the finish.

But Gunnar was pumping my hand, slapping my shoulder, sounding more excited than I'd ever heard him. "God, Mike! What a race! That was the best race I've seen in years. *Years!* I don't know what happened to you, but if it keeps happening, you're going to have to build a huge medal cabinet! That was just phenomenal! What guts! What heart! *What a race!*"

"Where's Derek?" I grated.

"He's at the hotel trying to warm up. I told him to use all the hot water in town if he wanted to. He broke his PR by twenty seconds. You broke yours by two minutes! Two minutes! God, what a gutsy race!"

The next morning before we left, the three of us were interviewed and photographed for an upcoming article in *Runner's World* magazine. It would be on newsstands by Valentine's Day, we were promised.

The first day back home, we slept in while Nebraska was buried under a thick blanket of white. The following day, we jogged as far as Gunnar's house where we mostly drank coffee, talked about running, and ate Shelley's Christmas cookies. On the way back to town, Derek said, "Too bad you can't see this. It's beautiful. Everything is white."

"I'm white," I said helpfully.

"Smart aleck," he chuckled. "Actually, you look a little rosy in comparison to the snow."

The third day after the marathon, Everly took me to her grandpa's place to help diagnose some kind of electrical problem in the water system.

This sounded like a bad idea to me. All my life, I'd been told that water and electricity don't mix.

When I pointed out this fact, she said she would explain it as we went. First we went to the tool shed to obtain some wrenches. She led me inside a massive metal building which was even colder inside than the air was outside where the sun had made a few brief appearances to try to heat up the wind-blown atmosphere.

After Everly propped open the door, we wove through a serpentine of machinery, mobile tool chests, and general junk. Less than a minute into our journey, the door slammed shut.

"Oh, crap," Everly muttered.

Standing behind her with my hand on her shoulder, I asked, "Does that mean we're locked in here?"

"No, it means it's totally pitch dark. Do you have your white stick with you?"

"Always," I replied jovially as I extracted my cane from my back pocket and snapped it open. "Where would you like to go?"

"Back to the door so I can prop it open and find the wrench I need."

"Borrow my shoulder, Madam, while I lead you out of this labyrinth."

I heard her sigh as she lightly put her hand on the back of my shoulder.

Tap. Tap. Tap. Tap. Tap. "Oops. Not that way. Let's try over here." Tap. Tap. Tap. I stopped. "Hey, I can't see a darned thing in here."

"Just find the door," she uttered.

Instead, I turned toward her and put my hands on her shoulders. "I think we're lost. Maybe we should get closer to each other to conserve body heat until someone comes to save us."

Her voice low and even, she asked, "Do you have any idea where my knee is in proximity to any body parts you may find special?"

"Ouch," I muttered. "Such naughty language."

Turning, I resumed reconnoitering a path to the door. Once there, I pushed it open and said, "Ah. Finally, I can see."

There were six automatic waterers in six different pens. Each waterer was made of hard plastic, was about knee-high and four feet by two feet with a ten-inch wide round hole in the middle where the animals could get a drink. Fitted inside each hole was a hard plastic ball which had to be depressed in order to reach the water.

Everly explained that the animals had to learn to push the ball down in order to drink.

"Sort of like learning to use a cup, eh?" I asked.

"I guess," she said in a tone indicating that my comment was stupid.

Each waterer was fed from an underground pipe. When an animal drank, the water level lowered and a float inside—much like the one in a toilet—dropped and allowed water to flow in from the pipe.

On each corner of each waterer was a screw that held the lid into the base. Using a half inch socket on a ratchet, Everly loosened each screw, and I followed her around the waterer turning each screw by hand until it stuck out a couple inches. Then we were able to lift off the lid.

She talked me through what she was doing next. "I have to unplug each heater and pull it out. Then I'll plug them back in one at a time, so we can figure out which one is tripping the breaker."

"Clear as mud," I responded. "What does the heater look like?"

"Here you go." She handed me a gizmo with a donut-shaped metal ring about five inches in diameter and an inch thick. Attached to the base of the donut was a four foot long electrical cord. "You actually stick this thing into the water?" I asked skeptically. "Doesn't it electrocute the cows?"

"Not if it's working properly," she answered. "But if it does short out, it trips the breaker. So it won't shock the cows, but it will allow the waterer to freeze."

"Hm," I grunted.

We went to the next waterer which involved slogging through the mud and two gates. It took fifteen minutes to get all of the waterers open and the heaters unplugged. Then we started back at the first one and reassembled the apparatus.

Because I slowed her down, Everly suggested that I wait at the waterer while she walked back to the power pole to flip the breaker back on. This was the pattern for the first four waterer heaters, all of which seemed to be working properly.

After she left me at the fifth waterer, I heard a distant rumble. The rumble was getting closer.

It was a herd of something. And it was coming fast. And it was coming straight toward me.

"Everly?" I called loudly.

If she replied, I couldn't hear her over the eternal wind.

"Everly!" I yelled. "EVERLY!"

I had no idea where to go or what to do as the hooves pounded toward me, shaking the ground.

Just before they hit me, I crouched and covered my head with my arms.

Then they were gone.

"They're on the other side of the fence," Everly called as she trotted toward me. "I closed the gate, so they wouldn't mess with the waterers while we had them open."

"I didn't know! I didn't know!" I shouted. Taking several deep, shaky breaths, I muttered, "I didn't know."

"I'm sorry," she said lightly. "I tried to tell you, but you couldn't hear me over the wind."

Shivering, I reached out until I felt the steel pipe fence only a couple feet from me. Leaning against it, I dropped my head and tried to control my pounding heart.

Something nudged my hand from the other side of the fence. I jerked away.

"It's Honu. Do you want to pet him?" Everly asked gently.

"No." My voice rising uncontrollably, I snapped, "If someone's going to kill me, I almost wish they'd just get it over with. I feel like there's a big cat toying with the blind mouse. I hate this!"

Back at the house that evening, I went to my room and changed into sweats and a better-smelling sweatshirt. While I was there, I heard Everly on the phone.

"We got them working. No problem. I guess there must have been condensation built up, and after I aired them out, they were fine. Either that or we let out the evil spirits. But everything was working when we left. No short circuits. No damaged heaters."

A minute later, she disconnected.

Then she went in her room and closed the door.

In the kitchen, I opened a jug from the refrigerator door and gave it a sniff. Definitely chocolate. After downing a large glassful and refilling the glass, I overheard a scrap of Everly's conversation.

"He's been keeping up a good façade, but today he had a little meltdown. I know it must be wearing on him. I don't know how much longer he can stay here."

Neither did I. I just wanted to run. Just wanted to race. Just wanted to be on the other end of the tether from Derek while our feet flew.

Taking the milk with me, I went to the piano. For the next twenty minutes, I banged out Beethoven. It was one of his later works. Written after he was deaf. It made for a good catharsis.

But I didn't quit there. After Beethoven, I slammed out a couple movements from one of Rachmaninov's symphonies. Then I did some improv of an old folk song with heavy soul undertones.

It was after midnight when I finally went to bed.

Oddly for me, I wanted a drink.

A week before Christmas, Derek and I were in the ballet studio attempting to do our balancing exercises—but mostly succeeding only in cracking stupid jokes and giggling—when his phone chirped. By now, I recognized that particular chirp as being from his wife.

It was time. Tish had gone into labor while shopping with her sister in Scottsbluff. The kids were already with her mom, so Derek grabbed his bag, told her he loved her, disconnected the call, and said, "Let's go!"

Fumbling on the wall hook for my jacket and my cane, I said, "You gonna drop me off at the house?"

"Hell, no, man. Last time, she was only in labor for forty-five minutes. It's a good half hour drive to Scottsbluff. We gotta pedal!"

Two and a half hours later, Derek padded up in front of me and asked brightly, "What the hell are you doing?"

I stopped weaving and faced him. "There are four air ducts in this room. Did you know that?"

He let out a long breath. Looking upward, he said, "I see two. Both in the ceiling. One to the left, one to the right."

"And one straight behind me ten feet. It's behind some sort of furniture. And there's another one to my right. About twelve feet away. See it?"

He was still looking upward. "Nope. You need to have your ears overhauled."

"They're on the floor," I pointed out. "Actually on the wall just above the floor."

He let out a guffaw and got down on his hands and knees. "Yep. Both of them are behind a long row of connected chairs." He stood. "The nurse told me to take a break."

"Does your wife get to take a break, too?"

He snorted. "Jeesh. You sound just like her. Man, that last contraction, she about busted my hand. I never dreamed it would take this long. Every pregnancy is different. Every delivery is different. I called Everly. She's on her way to pick you up."

"Oh, shucks. I was really having a great time sitting here without my phone, with no one to talk to, and not a single Braille magazine to be had."

"Yeah, I can tell you were really having a good time. You looked like Stevie Wonder."

I laughed. "He's taller than I."

With a snort, he said, "Yeah. Blacker, too."

"Really?" I asked innocently.

"I gotta go put my hand back in the vise now. Have fun analyzing the HVAC."

On the way back to the ranch, I asked Everly how the investigation was going.

As I expected, she said nothing.

I was starving when we got home. While Everly threw together some supper, I sat in the kitchen and waited. "We should have stopped at your mom's place," I lamented as my foot bobbed up and down. "I left my phone in the gym."

"You can live without it for one night," she stated with absolutely no sympathy.

"I should be reading the rest of those depositions and a couple of briefs." I let out a deep breath. "That smells good."

"It is," she replied.

"Hey, Kimberlyn told me I have weird facial expressions. What did she mean by that?" I probed.

"She's nuts, Mike. She tried to poison you with furniture wax. Why do you care what a psychopath thinks?"

"Well, I don't really care what she thinks. But I care if I look weird. So what was she talking about?" I pressed.

She didn't answer for so long that I decided she wasn't going to. But then she walked over to my chair and stood in front of me. "I'm going to touch your face."

"Okay."

With her fingers at the corners of my mouth, she gently pulled to the sides. "This is how sighted people smile." Then she pressed her fingers upward instead. "You smile with your whole face. With your cheeks. You squint when you laugh. Like a baby. For some reason in our culture, we learn to smile differently as we get older. I like your smile. Don't change it."

I put my hands on her hips. "Everly, are you sure you can't take a little break from your job? A short sabbatical, sort of?"

Backing away from me, she said, "Supper's ready."

The next morning, Derek showed up well before daylight. I asked about the baby.

"Boy. Eight pounds, six ounces. Baby and mom doing fine. I'll pick them up later today." Then he explained that he was not on foot. He had driven in his minivan.

"What's up?" I asked. "It's not slippery today."

"On the theory that if someone is watching for you, you shouldn't be where they expect you to be, we're going to run somewhere else today."

"Like where?" I solicited.

"Like forty miles from here."

Scowling, I asked, "What does Gunnar think?"

"It was his idea. Come on, let's go." He led the way to the porch. "One time in Synghalia, Gunnar lost a runner to kidnappers. After that, he was careful to vary the workouts and locations."

"Kidnappers?" I bleated. "No kidding?"

"Yeah. It seems that his runner belonged to one faction and the guys on the other side of the war didn't want him fighting. He was easy enough to find out there on the oval track. And since it seems like somebody has a target plastered on you, we're going to move our daily run."

"You don't like that target spilling over onto you?" I quipped.

"No," he agreed emphatically. "I don't. So we're going to see some new country."

"Promise?" I begged.

"Smart aleck," he grimaced when he grasped my pun. "I will get to see some new country anyway. You're still blind as a damned bat."

"Just where is this new country?" I probed.

We climbed into the minivan, and he turned the key. "Historical site. Scottsbluff. It was one of the stops on the—"

"On the Oregon, Mormon, and California Trails," I supplied. "Wait! Stop. I'll be right back." Hopping out, I trotted inside and returned a minute later.

"What was that all about?" he asked.

"I had to grab my National Parks Passport. I can get it stamped at the visitor's center. Let's go. Hey, maybe tomorrow we can tour Fort Laramie and the next day we can go to South Pass."

He snorted. "Maybe not. But from the top of Scottsbluff, we can see Court House Rock and Chimney Rock. Is that enough history for you for one day?"

330

I let him think about what he'd said. Then I plied, "You think I can see Courthouse Rock and Chimney Rock from Scottsbluff?"

"Just as well as you can see them from anywhere else," he stated. "You're still blind as a damned bat."

We parked at the base of the monument and walked inside the visitor's center. Aside from us, there was one ranger in the building. She welcomed us, stamped my National Parks Passport, and astutely noticed that I was blind. With my left hand on Derek's shoulder and my right hand holding a long white cane, I suppose it was fairly obvious.

The ranger apologized that not all of the signs were in Braille. But she did something for which I could have kissed her. She asked if I'd like to feel the topographical map of the valley.

We left the visitor's center and trotted up the paved roadway to the top of the bluff. Huffing and puffing when we reached the summit, Derek led the way to a lookout where he took my arm and pointed it to the southeast. "There's Chimney Rock."

"Is there a sign that points the right direction?" I inquired.

"Yep," he responded. "And you can see it. It looks like a toy from here."

I asked, "But you can't really see it, right?"

"Yes, I can."

"Twenty-three miles away?" I squeaked. "And you can actually see it? With your eyes? It's not just a photograph on a sign?"

"No, I can see it," he said calmly.

"I thought you could only see such great distances from the top of a mountain or something. This is just a bluff. I mean, we just ran up here from the ranger station. It wasn't that far."

While I marveled at the ability to see something so far away, he debated about whether we should run the trail down the bluff. In the end, he decided it would be safe enough, but there were places where we had to slow to a walk so that I neither fell off the cliff nor pushed him over it. The short cave portion of the trip was brutally chilling with the wind gusting through the tunnel.

We returned to the valley floor and put in several miles up the highway through Mitchell Pass.

After an unusually long silence, I repeated the words of my former running guide Charles. "Running provides a clarity of mind found in few other endeavors."

"That's not a well-kept secret," Derek panted in reply. "Covert Bailey said he once had a fight with his wife, so he went running. After a couple miles, he wasn't mad anymore. After ten miles, he couldn't remember what the fight was about."

"And after fifteen, he decided not to go home. I heard that speech, too," I said.

"Running does lend itself to deep thought," Derek avowed.

"It led me to another thought. Have you ever read a Louis L'Amour novel?" I asked.

He snorted. "I'm not a cowboy."

"Nor am I," I agreed. "But I learned something from him. When you're tracking a bad guy, sometimes there are no physical tracks. So you have to know where he is likely to go. Do you see what I mean? You don't read his footprints, you read his mind."

"Okay. So what?"

"So that's how I can figure out who is trying to do me harm. I have to figure out *why*. You think someone is trying to keep me from running. But why?"

He shrugged. "Beats me."

"No, think," I pressed. "What possible motive does someone have to keep me from running?"

"I don't know. It's a stupid idea," Derek answered.

"Maybe," I agreed. "But your point about the timing is pretty good. Even if somebody isn't trying to kill me, they're trying to distract me so I won't run as well. Who has something to gain by my not running?"

"Enemy back in California?" he offered.

I thought about that. Then I began relaying them aloud. Dolores Stoltz, who had pressed a frivolous case against me. Luther Dobson, who had tried to beat me up on the track. Carlos Burleson, who had raped and murdered Rosalee Kazemi.

Derek posed, "Which of them hated you before the plane crash?"

I scoffed, "You and my dad are the only people who think that plane crash was specifically intended to kill me. Sure, the bombers used my backpack. But that's because I was convenient. The convenient disabled guy."

"Paul Stuebbens," Derek offered. "He doesn't like you because you kick his butt every time he races you. Maybe his ego isn't big enough to take having a disabled guy kick his butt."

We had a good laugh over that one.

We planned another early morning run the next day. The forecasted temperatures were predicted to be below twenty with wind chills near zero Fahrenheit. As I was digging my warmest running tights from the dresser, something fell on the carpet. Fishing around, I picked up a chain with a medical alert charm affixed. Grinning, I said aloud, "Okay, Jennifer. Point well taken."

If I remembered later, I would send my sister a text and tell her she had subliminally reminded me to wear my charm today. Slipping the chain over my head, I continued adding layers of warm clothing.

Derek parked the minivan twenty miles north of town at a deserted intersection and we took off in the dark.

"I like it when we run in the dark," I mused.

"Are you nuts? I may never sire another child. My freakin' stones are gonna be stones by the time we make twelve miles."

"Maybe that's God's way of telling you four is enough," I offered.

"Speaking of babies, are you coming to the baptism tonight?"

My voice sounded funny because my cheeks were so cold. At least the month-old beard helped fend off some of the chill. "Sure. Everly's church is having some kind of shindig, too. I'll go eat there and then come and eat at your church. Surely I will get some kind of double godliness if I go to two churches in one day, right?"

He chuckled. "Something like that. So what's up with your heckler?"

"By *heckler*, are you referring to Dolores Stoltz or to whoever is trying to kill me?"

He replied, "Is there a difference?"

I thought about that. "Dolores is a hateful, vitriolic person, no doubt. But she's also not overly bright. She gets sloshed and calls to cuss me out, but she hardly possesses the mental faculties to mastermind a complex legal smear campaign. And unless she is the beneficiary of a recently departed wealthy decedent, she doesn't have the financial capacity. Which leads me back to the query: who's paying the tab on her legal crusade?"

I went on. "And for that matter, who paid Kimberlyn a car and a fancy Caribbean trip to poison me? Apparently the purveyor of the cash award made it clear that I was not to be killed. Just tortured a little."

"How much cash?"

"Hundred grand," I supplied.

He whistled. "Damn! Who do you know with that kind of money to throw around on something as ridiculous as making Mike miserable?"

"I don't know, but I'm losing my patience and enthusiasm for the prospect."

The air was still brisk and cold that night. Everly offered to drive me from her church to the K of C Hall, but it was only four blocks. I told her I would be fine.

As I tapped my way down the uneven sidewalk, I considered how much I had grown to appreciate my heavy, clunky, stiff cowboy boots. Laundry baskets were no match for the thick leather. Squishy cat toys were nothing. Heaved portions of sidewalk yielded no damage.

I never heard the car that struck me.

Chapter Fourteen
⠨⠝ ⠏⠜⠹ ⠀⠨⠗⠬⠃⠦⠲⠒

Sean Berry had been a Trooper for nine years. He was at the top of his profession—still fresh enough to enjoy the work, and experienced enough to have seen just about everything. So during his supper break as he was sitting in the parking lot of the truck stop, eating a takeout cheeseburger an hour past sunset, he noticed the sleek little black car that sped into the back of the lot without headlights.

Trooper Berry watched the little car drive up a ramp into the back of a panel truck that said Haskell Caskets on the side.

The search didn't take long. The driver seemed almost giddy to drop the tailgate to show the cop the back of his prize car.

The flavor of the encounter changed when, prompted by his earbud radio report of a hit and run in town, the cop asked to see the front of the car.

The crinkled quarter panel.

And the blood.

As I emerged into consciousness, I heard voices hovering over me. Most of the words were lost until someone mentioned that I was good on the piano.

For a fleeting moment, I wondered if this could be my eulogy.

But if it could be believed that pain ends with death, there was no way I was dead.

My entire body hurt, but the pain in my right leg masked everything else. It was so intense that I wasn't sure if my leg was still attached or if it had been wrenched off completely.

Gradually, I became aware that someone was holding my right hand and lightly caressing my upper arm. At some point, I heard myself mumble, "Everly?"

"I'm here," she said softly. Her voice was different.

I had to think about that for a while. Between the pain and the painkillers, my brain was soggy.

"Mike, you're going to be okay," she soothed. "Can you feel me holding your hand?"

"Yes," I croaked. My face hurt, and it was hard to speak. "Is my right leg gone?"

"No. It's still there." She sounded so different. So nice. Caring. Kindly.

Loving.

She was addressing me with the same tone she used with other people. The one she had only rarely afforded me.

That's when I knew I was dying.

Choking back that thought for a moment, I muttered, "What day is it?"

"It's Christmas Eve," she said softly. "About two in the morning."

I swallowed. Someone moaned. Probably me. "Everly, could you call Derek and tell him I can't run. I can't run, can I?"

"He knows where you are. He's praying for you."

She still sounded too nice to be addressing me.

"Would you please call my parents and tell them—"

"I've talked to them, too. They know you won't be flying in today."

I swallowed again. I felt slightly nauseous. Probably from whatever injury was killing me. "Tell them not to change their plans. Everyone will be home. Tell them to stay in California."

She squeezed my hand.

I couldn't think of anything else I needed her to do for me, so I asked, "Am I dying?"

She choked out a small laugh and sniffled. "No! You're going to be okay. You heal fast, right? You always tell me that."

"Then why are you being so nice to me?"

She sniffled again and let out a shaky breath. "Mike, the past six months have been the hardest I've ever put in for the FBI. Remaining professional and cool toward you has been tough. You are so warm and witty. You're the smartest person I've ever met." She let out another small laugh. "And you're awfully cute. But it's over now. I don't have to keep that wall between us now."

I wasn't tracking too well. "It's over? The bad guy is dead?"

"He's not dead, but he'll die behind bars. He'll never hurt you again, Mike, I promise."

"But he has so much money. What makes you think he can't get to me?" The blood pressure cuff on my arm inflated and slowly began deflating.

Everly spoke near my ear. "His motivation is gone. He'll never run another race on the outside. And he hit you with a car. That left—"

"Electric car?" I mumbled as I felt something warm going up the vein in my arm.

"Yes. It was an electric car. He hit you when you were crossing Seventh Street between the Methodist Church and the Catholic Church. Mike, with your leg broken, well, it means that. . . your running career is. . . compromised."

Addled though my brain was with pain and drugs, I interpreted "compromised" to mean "finished".

Whatever a nurse had put into my IV was making my head swim. "Sing," I mumbled.

There was silence. After a moment, Everly implored, "What are you trying to say?"

"Sing the song. About the maidens." I pressed my brain to remember the title of the song she had been humming all weekend. "Come All the Maidens," I prompted.

Everly pressed my hand again. In her clear, resonant alto, singing as softly as she could, she began.

> *Come all ye fair and tender maidens*
> *Take warning how you court young men*
> *They're like a star on a summer's morning*
> *First they'll appear and then they're gone.*

Her voice went quiet, leaving a void in the room, leaving only the beeping monitor beside the bed, the hissing air duct in the ceiling.

I squeezed her hand.

She resumed.

> *He'll tell to you some loving story*
> *He'll tell to you that his love is true*
> *Straightaway he'll go and love another*
> *And that's the love he had for you.*

> *Oh do you remember our days of courting*
> *When your head lay upon my breast?*
> *You could make me believe with the falling of your arm*
> *That the sun rose in the west.*

If I'd known before I courted
That love it was such a killing thing
I'd have locked my heart in a box of golden
And fastened it up with a silver pin.

If there was more of the song, I drifted off and missed it.

Late in the afternoon on Christmas Eve, I was transported by ambulance and plane to a bigger hospital. Then, on Christmas morning, two surgeons spent seven hours reconstructing my shattered and nearly severed right lower leg. It would be four more days before the doctors committed to whether or not the leg would remain part of me, and there would be four more months of surgeries.

Everly was right beside me for days. On New Year's Eve, she took a break for a couple hours. I was half-sitting on the bed when someone came into the room.

"Mike?" It was a man's voice. I had never heard it before.

"Yes?" I asked.

Sounding apologetic, he said, "Mike, my name is Paul Stuebbens." Then he clarified, "Senior. My son has run some races against you."

"Oh," I said dumbly.

"Mike, I. . . god, I can't believe this. I thought I was helping him reach for a goal he wanted, and all I was doing was. . ." His words trailed off. A moment later, with fresh resolve, he said, "Mike, I want you to know that you won't have any financial burdens resulting from this— this accident. I have put five million in a trust to cover any expenses you incur until you're back on your feet. I know I can't give you back the chance to compete in the Olympics. And I sure as hell wish you could have run and showed what you can do."

I was confused. "Mr. Stuebbens? I don't understand."

He was caught flat-footed. "Oh, god. You don't know? My son was driving the car that hit you. Hell, he's in jail now facing so many charges, he'll be lucky not to get the chair. I just can't believe he. . . Listen, I have to go now. My attorneys will be in touch with you regarding the trust account and how the money will be disbursed. If you need more, it'll be there."

Before I could respond, he was gone. No more than three seconds later, I heard Everly in the hallway, talking low. Her tone sounded ominous.

Then she burst into the room. With a heavy sigh of relief, she asked, "Are you okay?"

"Not really," I said. "My leg is broken. My arm is broken. My back feels like someone stuck a knife in my spine and gives it a twist every time I take a breath. I have two cracked ribs. And my right cheek is held together with stitches."

"Did someone come in and talk to you just now?"

"Yeah. Paul Stuebbens' dad."

"What did he tell you?"

"That his kid hit me and that he was going to pay for my medical bills and recovery."

"No kidding?" She pondered that for a while. "Between that and paying legal fees to keep his son from getting the death penalty, he's going to go broke."

"Really?"

"No, not really. He has plenty more where that came from," she mused.

"It was Paul Stuebbens who hit me? Why? And why didn't you tell me?"

She dropped onto a chair and said, "I'll answer your last question first. I thought you already knew."

"How could I?" I pleaded with all the volume I could muster. Which wasn't much.

She took a deep breath. "The night you got hit, you said he had so much money that you feared he would still hurt you from prison."

Raising my one good hand with the intention of rubbing my eyes, I somehow caught the IV tubing on something.

"Hang on." Everly stood and untangled the skinny plastic line. "And be careful of the stitches in your cheek."

"Don't worry. I can feel them," I emitted wryly. The eye-rubbing felt good. "Will the scar be hidden in my beard?"

She stood again and leaned close to me to scrutinize the sutures. "Yes. I think so. That's more than ten seconds."

Lowering my hand, I said, "What are you talking about?"

"You always rub your eyes for ten seconds. Before you go to sleep."

How did she know that? I knew I had never told her about the deal I'd made myself in college, the deal of rubbing my eyes for ten seconds every night. I had never told anyone.

Realization hit, and I asked, "Did you watch me go to bed every night?"

"I didn't watch," she said defensively. "I listened. You've taught me to be much better at listening, by the way."

I didn't let her off the hook. "You eavesdropped on me every night?"

"Not every night, no. But I wanted to know your patterns. The first few nights you were in Nebraska, I stood outside your door and listened. Partly to make sure you were doing okay, finding everything you needed and so on. I always heard that sound just before you got quiet. Exactly ten seconds. I couldn't figure out what you were doing, so one night, I watched you."

I gave a lopsided smile. It was the only way I could smile, due to the swelling and stitches on my right cheek. "Did you turn on the light or look at me with a flashlight?"

"You go to roost at night before the chickens do. It was still light out."

My smile dropped. "So why did Paul Stuebbens want me dead so badly?"

"Jealousy. Insanity. Spoiled brat. Take your pick."

"Did he do all the other things? The raft? Did he pay Kimberlyn?"

Beginning with a deep breath, she recited, "So far, he's admitted to poisoning your dog, bombing the plane—"

"You're kidding," I mumbled.

She sighed. "He was the guy in the hat and fake hair. The guy pretending to be blind. The woman was a flight attendant who, according to her supervisor, wasn't supposed to be on your flight. After she seated you and assembled the bomb, she apparently boarded her regularly scheduled flight to Hawaii. After that, she left the country on a chartered plane that landed in Singapore. She hasn't been heard of since. But before she left the US, her bank account mysteriously increased by a very large amount. Of course, the account was cleaned out hours before we started tracking her."

Everly continued. "Paul also says he hired Burleson to kidnap Rosalee Kazemi, tie her up, and leave her in your house. He swears he didn't tell Burleson to rape and kill her."

I cut her off. "Why Rosalee? Was she his preferred target? Or was she just in the wrong place at the wrong time?"

"Paul knew you were running with Charles, and he found out Charles' real name. A quick internet search was enough to inform him—so he thought—that Charles was a bona fide bad guy. So he thought if he paid someone to

343

kidnap Miss Kazemi, it would turn the entire Muslim brotherhood against you."

My heart was sick.

Everly wasn't finished. "Paul Junior also admitted to shooting the raft guide, paying Kimberlyn to make you sick, and hitting you with a car. By the way, you might like to know that Dolores Stoltz has dropped her lawsuit now that Paul Stuebbens isn't paying her legal fees. Prince Taylor is insisting that she issue a public apology to you and Gregg Horst and everyone else named in her cases."

A couple days later, I heard shuffling near the doorway.

"Mike? You awake?"

"Sure, Gunnar," I croaked.

"Are you up for a visit?" He was still hovering in the door.

Clearing my throat, I said, "Sure. In fact, I'm getting a little stir crazy."

Entering, he dragged a chair a few feet across the floor and said, "Mike, you know I'm not real good at. . . well, I'm not real good at anything but running. I never knew enough about cows to be a rancher. I guess to be honest, I never cared enough about cows to be a rancher. And I never really wanted to do anything but run. So I'm not real good at reading cues like hand gestures and facial expressions. My wife and daughter remind me of that frequently. They can both read a novel in someone's face in half a second. So if you don't want to talk about running, just say so. I'll understand."

"I want to talk about running," I assured him. "I'll always want to talk about running. I just won't be able to run for a few months. But I'll be back at it."

He was abruptly silent.

"But not for the Olympics," I added.

That seemed to reassure him that I wasn't totally delusional. Sounding more relaxed, he said, "I should probably tell you something else, too. Everly works for the FBI. She's an agent."

"I know. She was supposed to keep me safe. So that's why you invited me to run here. To get me out of California for a while."

"What? No. God, no! Mike, don't think for even a second that you were here for any reason other than the reason stated. Hell, Everly didn't even tell me she was coming here until I'd already invited you to train with Derek for a week. My offer had nothing to do with investigations or any of that stuff. But it did have to do with the fact that you're a damned good runner."

He crossed his legs and settled into the chair. "Last year I read about that first marathon you were in. The article talked about the guy who won the gold. His winning time was nothing spectacular. It was okay for a weekend runner, but nothing to write home about. But at the bottom of the piece, it mentioned the guy who *beat* the winner. I thought, 'What the hell?' and I tried to find some video. There wasn't any. So I saw your name again a few months later in a different race. There was video of that one. The whole race wasn't televised, but Derek and I dissected the footage we could find. You wore out five rabbits. Nearly killed the last one—and he was the previous years' NCAA Western Conference champion in the 10K! Man, that got my juices flowing.

"Then you ran that race in Podunk, Idaho, and cleaned up. I mean I could see you practically dragging your guide the last couple miles until you got to the pace vehicle. When he dropped off, it was like someone untied a lead weight from your shoes. You were flying!"

Wearing half a smile, I slurred, "I got to officially win that one because he was my only guide. I didn't have to switch off every few miles with a fresh one."

"It was a great race. Good strategy. Even splits. Incredible speed. It was a pleasure to watch."

"It was dangerous," I admitted. "I shouldn't have run without a tether."

"Why not? You won the race," he pleaded.

"It turned out okay because the street was so level. If there'd been a pothole, I'd have bought it."

Ignoring that, he said, "It was amazing to watch. Like I said, I don't know much about anything else, but I know a runner when I see one. So I figured if I could get you to put it all out there—really leave everything on the course—you could be outstanding. And in Montana, that's exactly what you did. God! That race was incredible."

Bittersweet.

I would never run like that again. And we both knew it.

Chapter Fifteen
⠨⠡⠀⠏⠿⠀⠐⠗⠐⠗⠮⠐⠺

In an interesting quirk of fate, I opted to stay in Nebraska during my recovery—even in light of an offer from Paul Stuebbens, Senior, to fly me back home in a reasonably comfortable medically-equipped jet. So after three weeks in the hospital, I returned to the same room I had occupied during training. Everly's aunt and uncle—both registered nurses in addition to being ranchers—took care of me, drove me to doctor and physical therapy appointments, and even to a couple of job interviews. Dad rigged up a way for Derek and me to talk to each other (tell raunchy jokes and laugh a lot) by phone during Derek's training runs.

Meanwhile, Everly returned to California to spend the next several months chasing paperwork to ensure that Paul Stuebbens, Junior, would remain in prison for the rest of his life. Because she had sublet her apartment when she went to Nebraska for an undetermined period of time, she had no place to live.

So I rented her my house. And my parents.

She ate breakfast with my folks on Sunday mornings. I forgot to ask if Dad took her through track workouts every morning before work.

Part of my convalescence was spent helping Charles set up an endowment for the Rosalee Kazemi Memorial Scholarship. Paul Stuebbens, Senior, eagerly agreed to donate the remainder of the medical trust he had set up for me. At first, Charles was uncertain whether the funds should be used to help future teachers, runners, or the disabled. In the end, we decided it would be doled out to anyone based on academic success and financial need.

I was still on crutches when I interviewed for the superintendent position in Tyler County, Kansas, a couple hours' drive south of Gunnar's place.

After the formal interview concluded, one of the board members asked what church I belonged to. Without a hitch, I responded, "I'm Methodist." Everly had asked if I would continue going to church when I got back to California.

She hadn't asked if I would continue going to church if I moved to Kansas.

By a four-to-one vote, I was hired. The elderly member of the school board who voted against me gave as his stated reason for dissent that he wasn't sure a city slicker could fit into the community.

Whether he really meant "city slicker" or "blind guy" was immaterial. I still got the job.

For what seemed to me a ridiculously tiny amount of money, I bought a huge, sprawling house and the quarter section of land on which it resided. The place was just across the street from the high school and my office.

For those of us who aren't children of farmers or ranchers, a quarter section of land is a hundred sixty acres! I felt like a member of the landed gentry.

A local well-known horse trainer set me up with a little Arabian mare who could run thirty miles in a day! He even trained her to watch out for overhead obstacles. She never once smacked my head into a tree.

Then again, there weren't many trees in my pasture.

Dad rigged up a way Derek and I could talk to each other (tell dirty jokes and giggle a lot) while Derek was running and I was galloping.

The most excitement in my first year happened three weeks into the fall semester when the music instructor failed to show up for fourth hour vocal music class. He normally taught at the grade school for two hours in the morning, and then drove to the high school.

I volunteered to babysit the choir until he arrived.

Later in the day, we learned that he had committed suicide in the parking lot of the grade school.

Thus, I inherited the high school vocal music program until a replacement could be found. (The teachers at the grade school worked out a rotating schedule to cover the elementary and middle school.)

The kids in the high school choir had already selected the score for their fall musical, but the casting was yet to be done. I took them through exercises to determine their individual ranges, moved several to different sections because they had been previously asked to hit notes they couldn't reasonably hit, and cast the roles.

A few of the teachers hesitantly approached me the day after casting. Apparently I had given the female lead to the "wrong" singer. Not only was she not a senior (she was a sophomore), but she was also from a broken home, her mother was a known drug addict and probably dealer, and she had no idea who her father was.

She also possessed a clear and sensational voice that was beyond compare in the small town ensemble.

Besides breaking tradition that the lead roles were to be assigned by seniority, I also suggested that if the kids were planning to work so hard to bring the play to the stage, they should extend their run. I tried for a second weekend of production but lost my bid due to an overly packed school schedule. Instead, we compromised with the Board and scheduled a Sunday matinee in addition to the Friday and Saturday evening performances.

We also beefed up advertising and increased ticket prices.

On the night of the first performance there was a malfunction with the mechanism that pulled back the main stage curtain. The maintenance man enlisted the aid of a couple of his buddies, and they thought they could have it fixed in twenty minutes.

It was already five minutes past the scheduled opening.

I had a thirty-second conference with two of the high school seniors. While one of them temporarily commandeered the lighting system, the other led me to the grand piano between the audience and the raised stage.

As he melted back into the darkness, I sat in the spotlight and fidgeted with the bench. Then I opened a piano book and placed it on the music stand.

A few people chuckled.

I turned a page and began playing a very stilted and stunted piece.

The auditorium got quiet.

I continued playing for half a minute, reached up and turned the page of music (more chuckles), and continued until the student who had led me to the piano walked up behind me, tapped my shoulder, and then pretended to whisper something in my ear.

I stopped playing. Turned my head toward him. Nodded thoughtfully.

He faded away again.

I grabbed the sheet music, flipped it upside down, and immediately started playing "The Flight of the Bumblebee".

The crowd exploded.

With a straight face, I finished the entire piece. Then I stood and held my hand above my eyes as though peering toward the main curtain.

With a shrug, I sat again and played a rousing Sousa's "Stars and Stripes". By the end, the whole audience was clapping.

Just as the applause died down, I heard thunder. That was the cue that we were back on schedule.

The kids performed magically. There were a few bungles, but they did a remarkable job of covering with improvisation. No one but a few parents who had critiqued them during the dress rehearsals noticed.

The piano routine at the opening was such a hit that the kids wanted to do it for the other two performances. Who was I to argue? Who doesn't like the spotlight? Even if I can't see it.

After the Sunday and final performance, I was standing in the hallway outside the auditorium as the audience filtered past offering congratulations to the cast. Keeping to one side so that my new guide dog Carlos could lay next to my left foot, I received a few pats on the back, but mostly I chatted with my veterinarian. She was the reason I had seventeen cats residing in my barn. So far, I had resisted the urge to take in her stray pound dogs, too. Carlos had only been with me for a couple months, and we needed to form a very strong bond before any other dogs interfered.

In the middle of a comparison of Science Diet versus IAMS pet food, I felt a slap on my shoulder.

"Hey, Brother!"

"Derek!" I returned. We shook hands and ended up in an embrace. "How've you been? What brings you down to the tropics of Kansas?"

Derek laughed. "Funny. It was twenty-nine degrees with a thirty mile an hour wind when we got here. But the answer is—"

The vet excused herself.

Derek continued. "We heard about the musical and came down to see if the new superintendent was any good as a choir director. Besides, Tish and I have not spent a night in a motel sans kids since our eldest was born."

Tish gave me a hug. After a hug from Shelley and a handshake from Gunnar, I invited them to join the cast for pizza—I had paid for the pizza, so I figured I could invite extra partakers.

"And you're all welcome to stay at my place tonight," I offered. "I have plenty of room for you. Heck, you could bring along your entire extended family. The place is huge."

Not surprisingly, Derek and Tish declined. But Shelley and Gunnar accepted.

And that's when I heard another familiar voice.

"Hi, Mike."

"Everly!" I burst. My reaction almost shocked me, but I had to restrain myself from saying, "God, I love you!"

Eventually, we retired to my house and shared a couple bottles of wine. When Derek and Tish left for their motel, Shelley and Gunnar turned in, and Everly sat next to me on the couch.

She took my glass of wine and before I could ask why, she kissed me.

During the lengthy kiss, my hands explored a good bit of her real estate. When I finally surfaced for air, I whispered, "Which bedroom do you want?"

"Yours."

I was on hand to cheer Derek across the finish line as he won Olympic silver four hundredths of a second behind a Synghalese runner whose dad/coach had won gold under Gunnar's tutelage twenty years earlier. Though I know he would have preferred the gold, Derek was four hundredths of a second behind brand new world and Olympic records. Dad and Gunnar both declared it was a "helluva race".

We celebrated that night in the Synghalese compound at the Olympic village. Those Africans sure knew how to throw a party!

Chapter Sixteen

⠠⠞⠓⠑ ⠠⠎⠊⠭⠞⠑⠑⠝

Four Years Later – Custer, Kansas

"Daddy, I can spell Mama's first name."

"You can?" I replied. "Let's hear it."

"E-v-e-r-l-y."

"Very good," I said to my firstborn. "Now spell Sandsebrotsky."

"S-a-n-d-s."

I waited, but it seemed she was finished. "That's only Sands. Where's the –brotsky part?"

She giggled her little three-year-old giggle. "Daddy, you always tell people it's too long, so they only need to remember the Sands part."

"We'll work on it later in the hotel. Are we almost to the stairway?"

"How do you always know?" she asked. "It's ten stairs up to the landing."

"Okay. Let's count."

One. Two. Three. Four. . . . In the middle of the flight of stairs, I noticed that she was tapping the toe of her tiny running shoes against the rise of each step. At the landing, I asked her about it.

She said simply, "I kick the step because you do it, Daddy."

"I do it because I'm blind," I reasoned. "It helps me know that my foot is all the way on the tread of the stair so I don't trip. You can see the steps, so you don't need to kick the back part."

"Oh. Okay. It's ten steps up to the next landing."

Again, we counted the steps. When we reached the top, she said, "Then I do it so if I get blind, I will already know how to go up the stairs without falling and hurting myself."

"I hope you never become blind," I issued.

"Why? You're blind, and you're a grown-up, and you're good at everything, Daddy."

"I can't drive," I reminded her.

"Yes, you can," she retorted. "Just not on the road."

"Don't you think it would be handy to be able to drive on the roads?" I posed. "Then we wouldn't have to call our friends in the middle of the night to drive us to the hospital."

She giggled and told me how many steps it was to the next landing. "Daddy, did it hurt this morning when Mama got Baby Brandon out of her tummy?"

"Yes, it did. My hand is still numb because she squeezed it so hard."

"Daddy!" she admonished. "You're silly!"

As we left the stairwell on the third floor, she tugged my hand slightly toward her so I didn't hit my shoulder on the doorjamb. I thanked her.

An hour later, we were on our way back across the big parking lot to the hotel where we were staying. She said, "Daddy, there must be something you can do better because you're blind."

I smiled. "Well, Sweetie, did I ever tell you about the time I was in a plane crash?"

Author's Note

A rough sketch of the character Mike Sands has lived in the attic of my mind for several decades since I read *If You Could See What I Hear* by Tom Sullivan. Because I simply couldn't know enough about Mike's world to do a credible job writing about him, I figured he would languish in my mental cobwebs and go to the grave with me.

However, last summer after I read a veterinary journal article about guide dogs, Mike elbowed his way into my mental parlor and demanded his own murder-mystery.

Educator and runner Mark McCowan, who navigates the world with his wife and running guide Stacy and his guide dog Arlo, was enthusiastically helpful from the beginning. It was Arlo who cracked this case when he wet on Mark's shoe at the pet relief area in an airport. Though the story initially made me chuckle (Mark described walking away: squeak, squeak, squeak), the event started the mental cogs turning and led to an explosive idea. Mark's friend Chris Lynch (runner and avid chocolate milk drinker) also provided much appreciated assistance.

Many thanks also to editors and proofers Pat O'Dell, Kendall Ottley, Annette Daniel, Diane Giefer, and Sandy Burkhard.

Made in the USA
Monee, IL
05 November 2021

81447101R10215